THE (… RS

BY *THE SAME AUTHOR*

THE PORRO PALAVER

THE OXFORD MURDERS

THE ISLAND OF DEATH

CROWNER'S QUEST

THE QUEEN'S HALL MURDER

THE CROCODILE CLUB

THE CAMBRIDGE MURDERS

BY

ADAM BROOME

Ostara Publishing

First published By Geoffrey Bles 1936

ISBN 9781906288075

A CIP reference is available from the British Library

Some of the words used and views expressed in this text, in common usage when originally published, could be considered offensive today. The Publishers have reproduced the text as published but would wish to emphasise that such words and terms in no way represent the views and opinions of the Publisher.

Printed and bound in the United Kingdom

Published by Ostara Publishing
13 King Coel Road
Lexden
Colchester
CO3 9AG

CONTENTS

CHAPTER I

TRAGEDY IN TRUMPINGTON STREET

It was a bright late October morning. There was a nip in the air, and the frost which had set in on the previous night was exceptionally severe for late autumn or early winter. There was optimistic talk amongst undergraduates and dons alike of skating on the Fens in a day or two—*if* the frosts held.

The great Hall of Trinity was crowded to capacity, for Sir Wedgwood Camberley, Regius Professor in Experimental Anthropology, was a popular lecturer and knew how to handle a subject, interesting in itself, in such a way as to maintain the attention of his hearers. Sir Wedgwood was always late for his lectures. He disliked beginning before his audience was fully assembled, and he had been known to pause for several minutes if a thoughtless undergraduate chanced heedlessly to interrupt his discourse once the doors of the hall had been closed.

He was tall, gaunt, uncouth looking, and there were traces of a Yorkshire accent in his speech which he made no attempt to conceal. He was in the early sixties, but looked younger, and the steely glare of his blue eyes was intensified by the great bushy greying eyebrows which overhung them. His hair was thin, and his complexion sallow. His dress was as untidy as that of a professor should proverbially be, and he clearly never made use of a magnificent trouser-press which had arrived one Christmas from generous, if critical, anonymous donors.

His lecture this morning was timed to begin at eleven. Professor Camberley had entered the Hall at five past, and at ten past still hung over the reading-stand serenely surveying his pupils, who waited with open books, pen and pencil in hand, to take his notes.

They were a motley throng, and amongst the predominating white faces there was a very fair sprinkling of black, olive, brown, yellow and even red. For at one of the tables nearest his lectern the Professor noted the hawk-nosed, black-eyed countenance of Chief Yellow Opossum, a Mohawk Indian of high rank who had matriculated at Trinity at the beginning of the term.

Aryans, Jews, negroes from West Africa, Indians from Bengal and the Punjab, Chinese and Japanese from the Far East—there was ample material in Camberley's congregation for practical demonstrations of the Professor's subject without recourse to the glass cases of the Anthropological Museum.

It was a world in miniature that the lecturer surveyed from his place on the raised dais, and as he waited for the last rustle of the students to subside he speculated on their individual futures in the great world without, and wondered, with some misgivings, how much use they would be likely to make of the material which it had taken him a lifetime of profound study to accumulate for their benefit.

For the space of a minute or so there was dead silence. But Professor Camberley seemed to delay longer than usual before making a start. He appeared to be lost in thought, and once more the brushing of gowns against benches and tables, the tapping of pencils on desks and note-books was heard in the Hall. Thoughts were wandering. The minds of the throng were turning towards the fens outside the town. Would the frost hold? Would there be skating to-morrow?

Professor Camberley woke all of a sudden from his reverie. He smoothed down the pages of the notebook open before him, cleared his throat and was about to begin. Pencils and pens were poised: thoughts reverted from the wintry countryside around to the sun-drenched plains and swamps of West Africa, where the lecturer had last, in thought, conveyed them. He had dealt with the effect upon the minds of the negroes of the mysteries of Nature around them, and how through the superstitions which their surroundings had implanted in their minds, their characters, so different from those of their white brethren of Europe, had been formed.

Fear was the dominating feature in their lives—fear of the forces of Nature—of the wild animals and ravening beasts around them—fear of the power of the white races which were shaping their destiny—fear of the spirits, gods and demons who lived in the trees, the rivers, the mountains of their ancestral land. This fear, in its turn, had bred hate and suspicion—poison of the mind—which the Christian missionaries of many denominations were trying to eradicate.

The Professor's hearers, putting aside the thoughts of skates and skating which had, but a moment ago, monopolised the whole of their thoughts, were ready to take down his conclusions on the effect of these factors on the characters of individual men, and thence on the nation as a whole.

"You may think, gentlemen," he began at last, to the accompaniment of a hundred pens and pencils scratching over the surfaces of as many note-books, "that we are wandering a little away from the beaten path of the academic anthropologist when we begin to talk of secret societies—clubs and the like. There are many who think—and some of them are very distinguished men—that once they have measured some skulls and investigated the question of diet of this tribe or that, they have done all they need towards the furthering of the ends of the science which they profess to serve. I have been called a heretic in the cause—gentlemen of this University who do not live a hundred miles from this College have accused me of having the mind of a sensational novelist, a criminologist—of trying to tickle the palate of the jaded seeker after new excitements and the like."

He paused for a moment, and continued:

"But isn't life like that? And isn't human nature the most interesting thing in this world we live in? And if we want to know all about anthropology—the science of man, more especially, as the dictionaries say—of man as a social animal—isn't it the abnormalities just as much as the normalities of the human being that should claim our attention?"

There was a murmur of approval which was stifled at its birth by a glance from the Professor's eyes under the shaggy, menacing brows. His hearers were as still as mice. The lecture promised to be even more interesting than usual.

And then, suddenly, a change came over Sir Wedgwood's features. They were animated, as before; but whereas the animation had previously been the obvious outcome of the interest which the lecturer felt in his subject, the expression which his hearers now detected in them was one of concentrated hate and loathing. A thrill went through the class as one after another of the students gathered in the Hall looked up to discover the cause of the pause in the Professor's discourse.

Sir Wedgwood did not move a muscle. But there was a twitching of the eyelids which caused his bushy eyebrows to quiver in an uncanny fashion. He looked, as a Trinity man said to a Clare man who was sitting next to him at the time, more like some wild beast of the jungle than a staid Professor of an academic subject in an ancient University. He seemed to be staring out away over the heads of his pupils before him. There was a sound as of a door opening, softly, and as the concourse turned stealthily round to find out exactly what was happening behind, an African student, wearing the gown of one of the larger Colleges, stepped awkwardly into the Hall and endeavoured to efface himself by slipping down on to one of the benches near the doorway which already held its full complement of undergraduates.

Almost as suddenly as it had appeared, the menacing look on the face of the lecturer vanished. The tension of those few moments had been great, and there was a general soft sigh of relief as the students turned once more to their note-books and prepared to take down the words of the unconventional don.

* * *

It was tea-time. In a cosy old-fashioned room on one of the top floors of Sidney Sussex College, Geoffrey Cranston, a third-year man, was entertaining a couple of friends from Trinity.

"It looks as if we'll get some skating after all. It's begun to freeze again already and the porter, who knows his Cambridge backwards, says it's sure to go on all night."

"Talk about freezing: one reads in books about people giving freezing glances and all that. But if ever there was such a thing in real life, I'd say old Camberley had it this morning when he was interrupted by the nigger from St. John's."

The speaker was one of his host's friends from Trinity. He and the other young man had both been with Geoffrey Cranston at Sir Wedgwood's lecture in the College Hall that morning.

There was silence as the gyp entered and made ready the tea—muffins and anchovy toast from the buttery were doubly welcome on the winter afternoon. When the three friends were left together once more the conversation again turned on the incident of the morning.

"I don't know what to make of it," said the host. "Of course, there's a wave of interest coming into the world again in spooks and spiritualism—I don't suppose you'd have to go so very far to find somebody or other somewhere who'd be quite ready to believe that there was something true behind all the old stories and yarns about were wolves and witches and vampires and all that," he ended somewhat lamely.

"I dare say; but I don't quite see what that has got to do with Camberley's looking daggers at a poor, unfortunate nigger who happened to be a few minutes late for his lecture this morning."

Pat Frimley was a matter-of-fact young man; and although he, like his two companions, was destined for the West African Civil Service when he had finished his time at the University, he was disinclined, with the positiveness of the young and inexperienced, to attach much weight to tales of the supernatural, even if they were concerned with the Dark Continent, with which he was so far unfamiliar.

"No more can I," put in the third undergraduate, Peter Bagshot. He had represented the University the year before in the ice-hockey match against Oxford. This had been played, owing to the uncongenial weather, on a rink in London. There was a chance that this year, with a real hard winter in prospect, the event might take place on natural ice in the open, and the anticipation of this possibility excited him much more than any amount of theorising and speculating on the magic which might, but which in his own opinion probably did not, exist in the Dark Continent.

"You two chaps are too damned matter-of-fact and cynical." Their host helped himself to a second buttered muffin, to show that an interest in the super-natural did not necessarily imply the possession of a mind above the appreciation of the more material creature comforts.

"I can't help thinking that when a fellow has dabbled, as we know Camberley has, in the history of secret societies and magic in Africa—or anywhere else, for that matter—for years and years, he's bound to begin to believe a little in the subject he's been teaching and studying for so many years."

"And what," said Pat Frimley, making further heavy inroads on the anchovy toast to proclaim his intense materialism to the world, "has that got to do with Camberley's giving the wretched Ogu Kalawa the frozen eye in Hall this morning? Surely it's quite easily explained in an ordinary way? Everybody knows the old chap's rabid about punctuality at lectures—especially his own lectures—and it doesn't seem to me that we've got to go to the supernatural to find an explanation for what happened this morning."

Geoffrey Cranston smiled—a smile of superiority.

"*You* saw the look in his eyes—on his face. Would *you* say that it was just a look of ordinary annoyance at being interrupted by an African fresher at the beginning of a lecture on anthropology?"

Frimley and Bagshot agreed that it was not, and their host went on to expound his theory further.

"It's my belief that Camberley's got the subject on the brain. He's read such a lot, investigated so much, written so many books, given so many lectures on what he calls metamorphic cannibalism—being able to change oneself into some sort of beast or reptile—that he's got to believe in it himself. He certainly *looked* like some sort of wild beast this morning—I think you'll grant me that—and it's my belief that he really *does* believe that in moments of intense passion or anger or what not a man can, and *does*, change into some sort of beast when he's got an account to settle with an enemy."

Cranston's remarks led to a heated discussion. His two guests agreed, as any of the others present that morning at the Professor's lecture must have done, that there was more than mere anger at an interruption in the old man's reception of the unfortunate negro who had disturbed his opening periods. But they were disinclined to read into the incident what seemed to them so far-fetched an explanation as their host wished them to accept.

"Do you know this fellow Kalawa?" asked Cranston when there was a momentary pause in the discussion.

"I do—pretty well," said Frimley. "Sat next to him once or twice during the first two weeks in term at some lectures at Emmanuel. As I could see that he came from the country to which we're all going, I got talking to him, and I've had him once or twice to coffee in my rooms after Hall. I didn't see that there'd be much harm in getting to know something about the place from someone who happened to be born there—even if he did happen to be as black as the Ace of Spades.

"He's rather a queer sort of chap," he continued, "very nervous, and full of all sorts of funny ideas. This is the first time he's left his own home, and I dare say he's finding everything here a bit strange—in fact, he said so. I dare say we shall find *his* country a bit on the queer side when we first get there. He seems to be afraid of something. He mentioned something about secret societies—the sort of shows that Camberley spoke about—and though he didn't actually say so, he gave me to think that he was in some sort of danger from one of them, though I couldn't make head or tail of what he was really driving at. He says he's the son of a chief—in Sierra Leone or Old Guinea—or one of those places—I can't remember quite which. There's another fellow in Cambridge from the same place—he's at Corpus, I think, though

I've never met him and don't know his name—and I gathered that, for some reason or other, Ogu Kalawa wasn't on speaking terms with him. They're both freshers," he concluded.

The discussion continued for a little longer, and was finally wound up by their host.

"Well, all I can say is that *I*—whether I believed in the supernatural or not—and, mind you, I don't say that I do—shouldn't feel specially comfortable about myself if anyone had given me the look that Camberley gave the wretched African in Trinity Hall this morning."

And the conversation turned to the more important topic of the possibility of a break in the weather.

* * *

"He's tight."

The two undergraduates had been up to London without the formality of getting "exeats" from their tutor. They were returning from the station to their rooms in Silver Street by way of Trumpington Street, and in passing down Brookside kept as far as possible in the shade of the trees opposite the Leys School, so as the more easily to avoid the possible attentions of the proctors on their final rounds of the town.

"Tight or not, we can't leave him there to drown."

One of the pair stopped in his hurried walk and stepped on to the grass verge which borders the stream at this point.

His companion also halted and listened. There came the sound of a faint groan from the waters of the brook.

"I say, come and help me get him out."

The two young men set to work with a will.

"Whoever he is, I believe he's dead."

The speaker's words were awestruck.

The limp body was hauled from the water, and two or three passers-by from the other side of the road crossed to investigate.

The body which the undergraduates had recovered from the brook was that of a young negro in a cap and gown which they recognised as belonging to St. John's College.

CHAPTER II

WHO KILLED OGU KALAWA?

"Is this exactly how you found the body?"

One of the young men who had made the tragic discovery had gone off post-haste to telephone to the police. But before he had reached a telephone kiosk, he had fallen in with Constable King of the Cambridge Police on his rounds down Trumpington Street.

"Not exactly, officer," replied the second of the undergraduates, Tom Mimbridge, of King's. The constable, unused to dealing with cases of homicide, had looked so suspiciously at his companion that he felt that he had better take on the responsibility of replying.

A little knot of curious passers-by had collected in a circle round the body which lay on the grass-plot beside the brook. Police-Constable King, feeling the responsibility of his office, waved them back.

"Will anyone here go and telephone for me to the Police Surgeon and then the police station?"

A couple of volunteers presented themselves.

"I've got a bike," said one of them, in the dungarees of a motor engineer on a night shift. "I'll go and fetch Dr. Greensmith if you like. He don't live far from here: I know the house."

With the approval of the policeman the man was off.

"And I will go and telephone to the station."

The new speaker appeared only just to have joined the group. His voice had a foreign intonation, and the constable gave him a searching glance before accepting his offer. The nearest street lamp was a few yards away, but King realised that the young man who had just spoken was an Indian or negro. The officer had the Englishman's not uncommon mistrust of the powers and intelligence of any foreigner, especially a coloured one, and hesitated for a moment before acquiescing.

He was just about to speak when, to his surprise, Tom Mimbridge, one of the undergraduates who had discovered the body, stepped forward from amongst the crowd.

"Excuse me, sir, but—but—I think that perhaps this gentleman had better stay for a moment. I'll go off myself for the police station message."

Constable King was more suspicious than ever. Why should this young fellow, whom he had found standing by the body when he had arrived with his friend, be so anxious to get away from the scene?

The foreigner who had made the offer made an uneasy movement. He seemed to be anxious to get off on his errand, and yet to hesitate to do so before the constable had made up his mind which man was to go. It was of no use for them both to go off on the same commission.

The policeman, who had not yet made any examination of the body, produced a note-book and pencil: the action gave him time to collect his thoughts.

"I don't know that it matters very much: only *someone* must go at once."

He spoke hesitatingly, as if confused.

Tom Mimbridge stepped briskly forward again.

"Excuse me, but don't you think you had better have a look at the body?"

The policeman's first reaction was resentment at what sounded like an attempt of the undergraduate to teach him his business. But as he did not feel by any means sure of himself, he suppressed the retort which he had at first decided to make.

"All in good time. I was just going to. But I think you know," he continued ponderously, "that it's most important that the Police Surgeon and the Inspector should be informed without delay."

"I know—I know," said Mimbridge impatiently, "but——"

He looked in the direction of the coloured man who had volunteered to go to the police station; the fellow seemed a little undecided, but he was, for all that, stealthily by inches backing out of the group which now, at a more respectful distance, surrounded the body.

"Ask him to stay till you've seen the body."

Mimbridge uttered the words in a whisper almost into the constable's ear.

"Excuse me, sir, but I want everybody to wait here just for a minute."

The engineer in the overalls had already gone off on his cycle. That was all to the good: the Police Surgeon would be on the spot all the sooner, and he would feel relieved when the responsibility for the next action rested not alone on his own shoulders. He had not the moral courage for the moment to address his warning to any particular member of the group. But he was impressed by Mimbridge's insistence, and though the thought flashed through his mind that this might be part of a tasteless "rag" perpetrated by frivolous members of the University for the purpose of having the laugh of the Force, he hastily brushed away the suggestion as soon as it occurred to his mind.

That decided the matter. The case looked a serious one, and none of the onlookers wished to bring suspicion on himself by appearing to wish to make himself scarce before the officer had concluded his enquiries.

Seeing that his orders had been obeyed, Police-Constable King stepped importantly forward and, flashing his electric lamp in the face of the figure which lay in a huddled heap on the ground before him, uttered a suppressed cry. He could see now the reason for Mimbridge's insistence. The victim was a man of colour, too. He had to make up his mind quickly. Mimbridge seemed a decent sort and was obviously willing to assist him. He stood up again to his full height and addressed the little crowd.

"I am afraid I must ask you *all* to stay until I have made an investigation: I may need your help." He had an inspiration. "You all know, of course, that a constable has the right to call upon any citizen to help him when a felony has occurred. And it looks as if there has been foul play here."

There was a certain pomposity in his tones as he quoted as nearly as possible the words of the official instructions given to him in the police classes which he had had to attend.

But there was still the problem of getting in touch with the Inspector.

"I shall be obliged, sir," he said, addressing Mimbridge, "if you will go at once to the police station, as fast as possible, and inform the Inspector in charge what has occurred."

The undergraduate began to move quickly from the crowd.

"But," called King after his retreating figure, "come back as soon as you've done so. I understand that it was you who, with this other gentleman, found the body, and I shall need to take your statement."

Mimbridge was off in the direction of King's Parade without further delay. The policeman looked anxiously around to make sure that the coloured man had not taken himself off. No, there he was, standing nervously fiddling with his fingers and straightening out his tie.

Constable King bent in a gingerly manner over the body on the grass before him.

"I understand you to say, sir," said he, addressing Mimbridge's companion, Ronald Windlesham, of King's, "that the body is not exactly as you found it."

"No," replied Windlesham, "it's not. We heard a sound—of a voice—from the brook there. We went and found this man in the water, and we pulled him out. I think he was just alive then. But now I think he's dead."

As the constable was digesting this statement and wondering what he was to do next, there was the sound of a car coming from the direction of Bateman Street. It swerved swiftly round the corner of Brookside and drew up abreast of the group round the body.

"Good evening, constable. I hear there's been some trouble."

Dr. Greensmith, a short, stout, active little man with a brisk manner, stepped from the car, just as the motor engineer who had summoned him reappeared from the darkness on his bicycle. Without losing time for further comment he went to the wet grass and bent over the body, whilst the constable held his lamp and the engineer his cycle headlight to help him in his examination.

"There's no doubt he's dead," said the doctor after a few moments. "And I don't think that this is a case of drowning."

He passed his hand over the wet clothes of the corpse and asked the bystanders to help him turn it over on its face.

"Hold your lamp a little nearer, please."

His order to the constable was sharp and peremptory. He had just removed his hand from the small of the back of the victim's body, and examined it carefully.

"Blood! Might have hit his *head* on a stone if he'd fallen into the water tight, but he'd scarcely have had a wound, through all his clothes, in the small of his back."

* * *

Inspector Worplesdon passed his hand wearily over his brow. He didn't like these night jobs, and the Fifth of November was not so very far off, when he'd certainly have to look forward to a further hectic night, though the work would be of a somewhat different sort.

"It's a bit early to get guessing yet."

Chief Constable Deepcut, who had been called from his bed as the result of the tragic discovery on Brookside, nodded.

"Greensmith is quite certain, since he examined the body carefully at the mortuary," continued Worplesdon, "that the death was due to a shot from a revolver—probably a small automatic—which penetrated the fellow's heart. He's positive that drowning was *not* the cause and he's also quite firm that the man wasn't tight."

"And have you definitely identified the man?" asked the Chief Constable.

"Quite." The Inspector yawned as he looked at the office clock, which showed that the hour was well past one in the morning. "He had a pocket-book with his name in it, and some cards. He's a fellow called Ogu Kalawa, of St. John's. We've called up the Dean already and found out that he was a freshman this term—from West Africa. He comes from a Colony called Old Guinea—not very far from Sierra Leone. Son of a chief—they all are, I believe—same as every Greek you meet is either a prince or the son or cousin or something of a king."

Deepcut nodded. "Well, I can't see that we can do very much more at this time of night. Didn't King say that there was another black fellow loafing around, too?"

"He did," replied Worplesdon. "He meant to take a statement from him, same as he did from all the others round about just after Mimbridge and the other chap found the body. But the funny thing is that he bolted. Must have got away while the doctor was examining the body."

The Chief Constable whistled.

"Sounds bad. We must find him. We must go into all the dead man's contacts to-morrow. It may be just a coincidence, though I must say it's a bit suggestive. I suppose in the end it will mean calling in the Yard. We don't often have murders in Cambridge—fortunately—and if we *don't* get to the bottom of it, there'll be no end of a kick-up in the Press—and in Parliament too, I suppose."

"There's something else that I got from King that seems to me a bit queer," said Worplesdon. He was beginning to revive in the warm police office, and he knew the importance of striking the right trail at once in a murder case. "We haven't seen this other chap yet. But King swears that they are as like as two peas."

The Chief Constable laughed.

"King's never been abroad. During the war the transport that I was in called in for a couple of days at Sierra Leone. I went ashore quite a while. I'd never seen niggers in the mass before, and on my word, I could never tell t'other from which."

The other shook his head.

"I thought of that, too—especially as King isn't the brightest spot in the Force—not by a long chalk. But he says that not only were they, to him, alike in face—and of course in colour—but they were about the same build."

The Chief Constable was not enthusiastic.

"*That's* nothing much to go on. As they're both Africans, they'd both be black. As King doesn't know anything about Africa, he at once assumes that they're just like each other."

"I'd thought of all that," said the Inspector, nettled. "But that's not what I meant. What I mean is that it isn't going to make our case any too easy—whether in *daylight*, and to anyone with any sense, they look as different from each other as Alexander and Mose. Of course, we haven't got as far yet as even suspecting what the motive may be. But what I *do* mean is that we may be up against a case of mistaken identity."

"You mean that perhaps the mysterious African was really after someone else and the St. John's man got bumped off by mistake?"

"That's just what I do mean," said Worplesdon.

"A fat lot of good *that'll* do us," said the Chief Constable sarcastically.

The telephone bell tinkled.

"I'll answer it," said Worplesdon, taking up the receiver which was closer to him on the table between the two men.

"Hullo! Yes? That you, Jenkins?"

The Chief Constable knew that Jenkins was the sergeant in charge of the station that night.

Worplesdon's features changed as he listened to the message coming from the other end of the line. The Chief Constable gathered that his companion, tired though he was with the exertions he had already endured that night, was excited and interested.

"All right. The Chief Constable's here and I'll report it to him. Send a man round to Corpus at once."

The name of the College pulled up Deepcut with a start.

The other put down the receiver.

"Things are beginning to hum with a vengeance The porter of Corpus has just rung up for someone to go round there at once. A black student has just been found there—shot—in his rooms, a fellow called Karifu Pompoli, from the same place as the other!"

CHAPTER III

BLACK MAGIC

"You look tired to-night, Daddy."

Sir Wedgwood Camberley nodded.

"I am tired, Dolly."

"Had a long day?" asked his daughter.

The Professor nodded again.

"Yes, my dear—a very long day. Lectures and meetings and——" He paused to yawn noisily.

"And you were out rather late last night, too, weren't you?"

The girl's father sat up in his easy-chair, before the comfortable fire in the old-fashioned drawing-room in his house in Park Terrace, as if he had been shot. He dropped the evening local paper which he had been reading as he sipped his after-dinner coffee, and covered his apparent confusion from his daughter by bending over the chair-arm to pick it up.

The Professor was a widower: his wife had died some six years since, and his only daughter, Dolly, now about twenty-two years old, acted as her father's housekeeper and secretary. She was a pretty girl—and clever—and had done very well in her last year at Newnham. He was extremely fond of her, but that did not prevent him from quarrelling violently at times with her in arguments concerned with his own subject, which was also one in which she had taken a diploma herself. Sir Wedgwood Camberley was fully aware of his own powers, and knew that his pre-eminence in the branch of science of which he was now Professor at Cambridge

University had not been obtained without being thoroughly well merited.

But this evening, rather to Dolly's astonishment, he did not seem at all pugnacious. He might at least, she thought, have quite legitimately asked her what business it was of hers to pry into his private comings and goings. But he didn't. He picked up the paper again, smoothed it out on his knee, and sipped some more of the coffee which stood, in a dainty egg-shell china cup, on the little Victorian table by the side of his chair.

"I was, my dear—quite late—much later than I should have been, considering the work that I knew I had got to-day before me. But it couldn't be helped."

He became silent again. Dolly Camberley, leaving her own easy-chair which faced her father's before the cosy fire, came across to the Professor's and placed her hand gently upon his brow.

"You know—you look *awfully* tired—Dad—awfully tired. And I think you really ought to go to bed early."

She quite expected an outburst: to be told, as she had been told before, that what her father chose to do was no business of hers; that modern children were a good deal more officious than they ought to be, and had a better idea of what their elders should do than they had themselves. To her surprise, there was no momentary flash of anger in the shaggy-browed eyes which looked up into hers. The lines of his worn face looked deeper than usual, as if he were in need of sleep and rest.

"I know I ought, my dear—I know I ought. But unfortunately I can't—and so that's that."

As he spoke the last words there was a note of defiance in his voice: he wasn't going to be ordered about by a little chit of a girl who ought to be minding her own business.

But Dolly was determined. She was *petite*, but sturdy, and the Professor saw in her blue eyes—so like her mother's—the signs of a will as strong as his own, signs which were repeated in the firm lines of her pretty, well-modelled chin, and the finely chis-elled curves of her little mouth.

Sir Wedgwood saw that the explanation which he had given would not satisfy his exacting young daughter. She was going to speak again, and he quickly got out his own words before she was able to frame her thoughts.

"My dear," he continued, "I've to give the third of a very important series of lectures to-morrow in the Hall at Trinity, and I haven't finished preparing it. I thought it was all right. But I've been thinking things over and a new line of thought has been suggested to me. I think you know by now"—he smiled grimly—"that I'm not one of those men who go on, term after term, year in, year out, droning out the same lectures over and over again without the change of a word or phrase since they were first elected to their Chairs, and without taking the trouble to keep themselves abreast of modern discoveries in their subjects, and do their duty by the pupils whose parents pay for them to listen to them."

He shook his head violently. He was reviving now that he had begun to ride one of his pet hobby-horses. The great head, with its mass of untidy hair, was looking leonine again, and Dolly saw that it would need a struggle on her part if she were going to enforce her will upon her obstinate father.

She appeared to give up the attack: it was no use trying to argue with the Professor if he were getting into one of his stubborn moods. She must prepare to accept defeat for the time being and try to attain her objective later by less direct means.

"Very well, Dad, that's enough. You ought to know by now what you can do and what you can't—and what is best for you. Only I think you ought to rest a bit, anyway, in your chair here by the fire, before you begin anything like work. You know you won't be at your best if you try before you feel refreshed again."

She bent down over her father's chair, kissed him tenderly on the mouth, and went back to her own.

"Anything in the paper? I see—on the bills—something about a double murder—undergraduates."

Again the startled, hunted look came into her father's eyes. She could not understand it at all. What was the matter with him this evening? He must have been overworking—probably sat up most of last night, after he had come in so late—and his nerves were worn to fiddle-strings.

The Professor appeared to regain his calm when he replied.

"Yes," he said, "a terrible thing. Two young Africans—one from Corpus and the other from St. John's, both killed, and both, so it seems, in the same way"—he referred again to the columns of the newspaper—"and within an hour or so of each other—the one in the street—in Trumpington Street—near Brookside—and the other in his own room in College."

It was the girl's turn to express astonishment.

"Oh," she cried excitedly, "what were their names? I know—you know—Pat Frimley from Trinity? *He's* going out to West Africa next year—and he told me he knew a black man from somewhere out there who came up as a fresher this term. He pointed him out to me one day in the street. He even introduced me. He said the man was quite a good sort."

"One of the fellows' names was"—he referred again to the paper—"Kalawa—Ogu Kalawa—he's the St. John's man—he——"

"Oh," exclaimed Dolly, "why, that was the name of this man. How awful! Coming all the way from Africa to this country—where everything is so safe—and then getting murdered. It's too awful."

Dolly was a matter-of-fact girl, not given to expressing her emotions publicly, but a tear came into her eye as she dwelt for a moment on the picture of the unfortunate young African, coming to Cambridge full of hopes and ambitions, having braved the dangers which she had heard of in the Dark Continent, only to fall a victim to a murderous attempt in Cambridge.

Her father ignored this display of sentiment.

"When, my dear," said he coldly, all his perturbation of a few moments before completely vanished, "you know as much about the negro population of West Africa as I do, you'll waste less time on pitying them. I've not been to their country yet—it's not absolutely necessary for an anthropologist to go to the spot whence his material is drawn—but when you've read as much as I have of their loathsome, bestial customs and so-called religions you'll spare yourself the trouble of wasting your pity on them."

The Professor was on familiar ground: his daughter had heard him talk like this before, though never with quite as much venom as he now infused into his words. His motto was, and always had been: "East is East and West is West—and never the twain shall meet." She knew that he strongly deprecated the mixing of the coloured races with the white in the Colleges and University. An Englishman's home was no longer his own: it was invaded by all sorts of barbarians, in search of a little veneer of polish to impress their fellows when they returned to their bush hovels in the countries from which they had come, and the minds of the English youth—male and female—with whom they came into contact, were in danger of being corrupted by the heathenish superstitions and beliefs which were being imported into their midst.

She always thought him a little unfair when he went on in this strain, and had often pulled him up. But he invariably became so heated when the question was discussed that she had of late refrained from forcing him to continue the argument. She had heard it said, of the cases of other great men, that they all had their weaknesses and their obstinacies which no amount of the argument and thought which they were in the habit of giving to other subjects would remove. She had heard of distinguished scientists, whose custom in their own spheres was to weigh and sift every atom of evidence before allowing the smallest alleged fact to stand as proved, who were quite susceptible to being deceived by the most palpable and obvious frauds and impostures when they developed a taste for dabbling in the mysteries of the spirit world.

The present occasion was a little unusual, for it hardly seemed decent, to say the least of it, for her father to give unbridled rein to his pet prejudices on the subject of the intermixing of the white and coloured races at a time when, from all accounts, two unoffending African undergraduates had just met their deaths in the University town at the hands of unknown murderers. Hard as she found it to put a curb upon her tongue in defence of the rights of the strangers who sojourned within the University's gates, she decided that she would refrain from provoking the unhappy argument further. Her father was tired and over-wrought. No good could come of any attempt to thwart him in his present mood, and he would expend the energy which he so badly needed for more important things in a violent effort to convert her to his views.

"I know—I know," she said quietly. "But how did these men get killed? Have they caught the murderers?"

The Professor grinned sardonically: the expression in his eyes as he spoke was almost devilish.

"No, my dear, no—they haven't," he answered, speaking very slowly and cutting off each word very distinctly from the other. "And," he added, "I sincerely hope—they—never—will!"

Accustomed as she was to the Professor's absurd prejudices, Dolly was astounded at the spite which her father infused into his tones. It was almost as if some spirit—some evil demon—had entered into the man who, as she knew, could be so kind and gentle, and who would not, in his saner moments, hurt even a fly.

But she dared not ask him why. There couldn't, she thought, be a convincing answer to such a question. She waited for him to continue: it was better to let this unreasonable, inhuman mood of his abate of its own accord.

"Devils—*devils*," he almost hissed out the words. "They have only got their deserts."

For a moment or two Dolly almost feared for her father's sanity: his expression was not good to look upon. His face was distorted with the bitterness of his feelings, and he threw the paper from him as if it were some unclean thing.

* * *

The rest of the evening had passed off uneventfully. Sir Wedgwood had gone off into his study to get on with his work, promising, however, that he would go to bed early. She knew that his ideas of time, when he was deep in study, were somewhat vague, and determined to stay up till after eleven so that she would have the pretext of going into his study to say good night to him before herself going to bed, and possibly, if she found him in a more reasonable mood and sufficiently fatigued, of persuading him to follow her example.

When the Professor had retired to his study across the hall, she picked up the paper, and read all that was known as yet of the two mysterious deaths. The second man, the undergraduate at Corpus, appeared to have met his death in the same way as Ogu Kalawa—by a shot from a small automatic pistol.

The old grandfather clock in the dining-room chimed eleven. There was still no sound of the door of the study opening: the Professor was still at work, still unheeding of his promise to his daughter. She would give him five minutes and then beard the lion in his den.

The clock was chiming the quarter when she next looked up from the book she was reading. Softly she tiptoed across the hall. She tapped gently before opening the door. Her father was bending over his desk with his back towards her. As he heard her footstep, he started and turned round. There was something in his right hand—something which he had been examining. In his surprise at seeing her so unexpectedly the muscles of his hand relaxed. A small object fell to the floor. The rays of the desk lamp fell upon it and it returned the light from a polished surface.

The thing which her father had dropped was a small automatic pistol.

CHAPTER IV

THE PROFESSOR EXPLAINS

For a moment neither the Professor nor his daughter was able to speak. Dolly felt her heart beat violently, and her breath came in gasps. She felt giddy, and as she reached for a chair near the door her father stepped quickly forward to save her from falling.

"Why—what's the matter, Dolly? Here, just lie down on the couch till I go and fetch you a little brandy."

Sir Wedgwood carried the limp form of the girl to the sofa and was about to go on his errand. But Dolly clutched wildly at his coat-sleeve.

"Don't go—Daddy—don't go. I'm all right—shall be in a minute. I don't want any brandy—only—only——"

She closed her eyes and seemed unable to speak.

The Professor, any fierceness that there might have been in his eyes completely vanished, bent over his daughter and kissed her gently on the forehead. When she opened her eyes again she was astonished to see that he was looking completely puzzled. She could not help laughing, though to the Professor her laugh sounded a little hysterical. He looked more perplexed than ever.

"Why, Dolly? What has come over you? You gave me a fright, but you seem to have had a worse one yourself."

The girl closed her eyes again to give herself time to think. But when she did so the thoughts that would keep on coming into her brain were not pleasant ones, and they frightened her. The baffled look upon her father's face had almost convinced her that the suspicions which had sprung into her mind as she entered the room and saw him drop the automatic pistol were all nonsense. If he had been guilty of what she had at first imagined, how could he look at her with those innocent, bewildered eyes? Only an actor of consummate skill, she told herself, could have counterfeited at that moment such complete ignorance of the nature of his daughter's thoughts and suspicions. And Sir Wedgwood was anything but good at hiding his feelings. It was, rather, one of his faults that he never made any attempt to do so; and many were the misunderstandings and coldnesses which he had caused amongst his friends and acquaintances by his habit of calling a spade a spade and of not trying in the least degree to cause his face to hide his feelings and emotions.

She felt herself go hot and cold all over as she opened her eyes again and looked into the anxious face of her father as he bent over her, felt her pulse and gently stroked her brow. For she had suspected, for a moment, if for a moment only, that her father was a murderer.

Of course, the thought was absurd: she must be going mad if she could ever dream of accusing him of committing so foul a crime, shooting a harmless African in the back in the streets of the University town.

"I—I—I don't know what to say. Only—only—somehow I got such a fright when I opened the door and you—you—dropped *that*."

To her surprise and to her intense relief her father, hearing her words, gave a look of astonishment and then, throwing back his head, burst into a noisy guffaw.

"My good girl—*what* was there to frighten you in that? Did you think that I might perhaps be a *murderer?*"

Dolly blushed again as he formulated her thoughts in plain words.

"'Pon my soul—I believe you really did."

Sir Wedgwood was now quite himself again, and clearly much relieved. He turned away for a moment and, stooping down, picked up the small automatic from the place where it had fallen upon the floor at his daughter's sudden entry.

Dolly could have cried for joy. Her father's attitude, when he realised what it was that had so upset his daughter, completely freed her mind from the fantastic suspicions which she had conceived. Had there been any sort of foundation for what she had for the moment expected, the very last thing that anyone in the Professor's position would have done would be to pick up the very evidence of the crime which he was supposed to have committed.

"Never seen a pistol so close before?"

He held the small shining weapon in the rays of the reading-lamp, and its brightly polished barrel gleamed wickedly in the light.

Dolly, relieved though she was, shuddered a little. Even if Sir Wedgwood was as innocent as she now felt sure that he was, a thing like that—if the reports in the papers were correct—had been responsible for sending two unoffending African students to an early death on the preceding night.

"You didn't know I had one?"

Dolly shook her head weakly. She was beginning to feel ashamed of herself for her foolishness.

"I haven't had it very long. I bought it at the beginning of the term—soon after I heard that there was a chance of my going for a tour in West Africa to do a little practical anthropology amongst the blacks. But I didn't tell you—didn't show it to you. I know that women—I don't know why—are always supposed to be afraid of fire-arms—and there didn't seem any need—anyway."

The ending was lame, and fresh suspicions began to crowd into the girl's mind. He seemed to be making excuses for himself. Why should he if he had done nothing of which he had any cause to be ashamed or to be afraid?

Professor Camberley sat down in the arm-chair by the side of the couch on which his daughter still lay.

"I dare say you'll laugh—and call me an old woman: though why an old woman I don't quite know, seeing that, in my experience, they're no more foolish as a rule than old men, and often a good deal more sensible."

He seemed to be talking in rather a random way and Dolly's fears refused to be entirely allayed.

"The fact is that after that affair last night I began to feel just a bit nervous about myself. I'm often about the town—late—and if one perfectly innocent human being can be suddenly bumped off—as they say—like that—why shouldn't another?"

Dolly nodded. But her father's words only had the effect of redoubling her suspicions. There were *two* tragedies the night before—not merely one: and he *had* been out that night himself, about the time the murder must have occurred. Why should he refer only to the *one* case, unless there were some special reason for its being impressed upon his mind? And why should he be handling the revolver at home in his study to-night? He wasn't going out, and there seemed to be no reason for his action.

There *would* be a reason for doing it—*if* it had been used. It would need to be cleaned. She almost went off again into a faint as she realised the complexion which such an explanation would put upon her father's actions.

But he seemed now to be perfectly collected.

"I'd never really troubled to have a good look at the thing before. It was in the drawer of my desk here—locked—and I happened to turn it up when I was rummaging around for a note-book I couldn't find."

He got up once more and came and bent over his daughter again.

"There, there——" He still did not seem to guess what she had been thinking—or else—being guilty—he was trying to pass the matter off as lightly as he could.

The moment the thought entered her head she was ashamed of it, and felt herself blushing again to the roots of her hair. She was glad that the rays of the lamp did not fall directly upon her face and that her reactions were hidden from her father.

Suddenly the Professor's tones became grave again.

"I'm sorry, my dear, that I gave you such a start. But I hope you'll see how unnecessary it was to be frightened. The thing's not even loaded."

He bent a little nearer to her face as she lay, still perturbed and anxious, upon the couch. His next words were spoken more softly, and with a graver intonation.

"But I'd rather—my dear—that you didn't say anything about the pistol to *anybody.* The police are an interfering lot, and I've got to confess that I haven't got a licence."

The words sent a shiver through Dolly's spine. She felt, somehow, that her father was not speaking the truth. He did not want the police to know that he had an automatic pistol. Why? His own explanation was too trivial to be true: she could not believe it. As the true significance of her thoughts was borne in upon her she realised that, if she were right, her father *was* a murderer!

With a little cry of pain and horror Dolly Camberley fell back in a swoon.

CHAPTER V

A DEAD END

"WELL," said the Chief Constable wearily as he helped himself to a cigarette, "I'm afraid it'll mean we'll have to call in the Yard after all."

"I agree with you," said Inspector Worplesdon, pulling out a pipe.

The inquest on the two coloured undergraduates, who had each met his death on the same night, one in the public streets of the town, and the other in his own rooms in College, had just been concluded in the Coroner's court. The cause of the death had been the same in each case—a shot fired, at close quarters, into the back, from a small automatic pistol whose make and calibre had been identified by a local gunsmith, called in by the police for the purpose. The verdict had been the same in each case, of "Wilful murder against some person or persons unknown."

"It's difficult to say which is the more puzzling of the two," said the Chief Constable. "It looks as if the fellow Pompoli in Corpus was killed first. For the other one, Kalawa, was found at about eleven-thirty—the time's fixed by the time the nine-fifty-five from King's Cross came in with the two chaps who'd been up to town without exeats. He was alive when they found him, and though he couldn't say anything coherent, he couldn't have lived long in the brook after he'd been, as I suppose he was, pushed in by the murderer, weak and shattered by the shot that finished him off."

"In the other case," broke in Worplesdon, "we've not only got the doctor's evidence that the man had been dead about two hours, but there's the evidence of the Corpus porter, who saw him post a letter in the Lodge almost as soon as Hall was over, telling him that he was going back to his rooms to work. There's no chance of any outsiders being admitted to the College after nine, so if it was someone outside the College who did it, he must have been in before then and out before midnight. Probably quite a few minutes before midnight, anyway, as if he was a 'Varsity man, as we must suppose he was, he'd have to be back in his own rooms by then. And he wouldn't, knowing what he'd done, risk bringing any notice upon himself by being late and having to explain where he'd been and what he'd been doing at that time."

"That's so," said Deepcut. "But there's always the possibility that it was actually a member of the College—or one of the staff, if we want to cover all possibilities—who murdered Pompoli. And there'd be no sort of check on him as far as getting out of College was concerned."

"And the porter can't, naturally, swear to all the strangers he let out that night who'd been visiting friends in Corpus. He remembers the faces of a few—three Pembroke men—Johnson, Crawford and Sanders. Three from Christ's—one, another black man—Swainson, Brimshot and Weybridge—Cranston of Sidney—a lot from Trinity—he can place four or five of them——" The Inspector glanced at a pocket-book on the table before him to refresh his memory. "I see the names he gives are Purley, Frimley, Smithson and Bagshot."

He closed the book with a snap and a sigh.

"But what's the use of going on? Half the under-graduates of three-quarters of the Colleges in Cambridge seem to have spent the evening in Corpus that night!"

Despite the seriousness of the Inspector's plight, the Chief Constable laughed.

"Well, it'll keep your fellows busy taking statements and tracing contacts. It's not often they get a job like this. It isn't very common for two people, both undergraduates, to get murdered here in one night, one in his college and the other in the street. And as for two niggers—bless me—it seems like a dream!"

"A *nightmare*, you mean," said Worplesdon without a gleam of humour in his eyes. He didn't like the way the other man was taking the matter. He was Chief Constable—*he* wouldn't have to do all the donkey work which the Inspector knew that this case was bound to involve.

"I'm sorry, Worplesdon; I was only chaffing. I *know* what a serious business this is going to be. But I always think myself that when one thing happens after another and one's troubles multiply in this way, it makes one feel sort of light-hearted. The sheer impossibility of dealing with them all at once and satisfactorily seems to make the thing easier somehow. One knows that one can't do impossibilities, and one doesn't try. But if it's only *one* hard nut to crack, a fellow sort of concentrates on it and realises that he really *is* up against it."

Even after this explanation, not very lucidly conveyed by his superior, the Inspector was not mollified, though he dared not make too open a declaration of his feelings.

Chief Constable Deepcut was entirely serious again. He had no intention of wounding the feelings of the Inspector, who was, if stolid and rather slow in the uptake, an excellent worker once he had been put on a scent, though he had not usually the initiative to pick up the trail himself.

"I'm afraid, all the same, Worplesdon, that that's exactly what will have to be done. We shall have to begin on the fellows whose names the porter happens to remember. From them we may be able to get a line on the other strangers who were in Corpus that evening and whom he cannot place. It shouldn't be quite so difficult as it seemed at first, though it will mean a lot of slow and tedious work."

"But as you suggested before—even that isn't the end of it. We can't know, at this stage, if it wasn't actually someone inside the College itself. It seems to me it will mean interviewing every member of the College and staff as well as just the strangers who happened to be in on a visit."

The Chief Constable nodded.

"That's true. Only I didn't want to pile on the agony at the start, seeing how you were taking the whole affair. And another thing that makes me think we'll have to call in London is the nationality of the two victims. It's difficult to believe that these deaths are merely a local affair. These two fellows came from three thousand miles away—West Africa.

"The clues—when we pick them up, if we ever do—are just as likely to be out there—or anywhere else in the world, for that matter—as here. As soon as one thinks of West Africa one's mind jumps to thoughts of secret societies and clubs—at least, *mine* does."

"You mean," put in the Inspector, showing a little more interest and animation, "that these murders may be political affairs, or mixed up with ju-ju, or magic, or voodoo, or whatever they call it?"

The Chief Constable nodded.

"That's just what I do mean. I know it sounds rather like a story-book; but then, story-books would never come to be written if the things in them weren't suggested to the people who write them by things that *do* happen."

On second thoughts the Inspector didn't see any particular cause for jubilation in the suggestion that the Chief Constable had made. The thing was going to be quite hard enough without having a dash of magic or voodoo thrown in.

There was reason for Worplesdon's perturbation and perplexity. The enquiry at the Coroner's court had thrown no light on the mystery of the strange deaths of the two African undergraduates. Ogu Kalawa had been seen after Hall at St. John's by a number of young men of his own College, reading a paper in the Junior Combination Room. He was quite popular with his fellow undergraduates, and they had asked him to come up to the rooms of a man called Raynes, in College, to do some of the African conjuring tricks at which he had shown himself an adept. He had refused, politely, and given as his reason that he was going to see another African—a third-year man from Nigeria—who lived in rooms down the Trumpington Road, and to go over some lecture notes of the past year which his friend had promised to give him. The porter was able to confirm that he left the College at a few minutes before nine. He had laughingly told the porter that the evening would be an expensive one for him, as he would not be back till pretty late, and would be obliged to incur a gate fine.

His Nigerian friend had been interviewed by the police and confirmed the story which Kalawa had told the porter. The St. John's man had reached his rooms at about a quarter past nine and stayed till about 11.15. The Nigerian's landlady, Mrs. Smithers, being separately questioned by the police, had corroborated. Her lodger had been in all the evening. She had heard him dictating what were presumably the promised notes in his sitting-room to his friend in a monotonous voice which she remembered as having annoyed her husband, who had been listening-in, in the next room, to a play on his very inefficient and almost inaudible wireless. She had herself let out Mr. Kalawa, whom she knew well by sight as a frequent visitor to her lodger, and locked the door behind him. She had herself seen the Nigerian go off upstairs to bed after bidding her good night. She did not go to bed herself that night until well after midnight, and as she had passed the door of her African lodger she heard loud snores proceeding from his room and had no doubt that he was sound asleep.

That, and the stories of Mimbridge and Windlesham, were all that the police had so far to go upon in connection with the mysterious death of Ogu Kalawa.

The case of the other young man, Karifu Pompoli, was just as unsatisfactory from the police point of view. No one who had come forward had seen him between the time when he had posted his letter in the Lodge letter-box and said good night to the porter and the time when, between 12.30 and 1 a.m., he had been found dead in his bedroom. He occupied a set of rooms on the first floor of the Front Court. He was of a retiring, shy disposition, and the other undergraduates who lived on his stair had told the police that he took his studies very seriously and regularly retired to his room after Hall to study. He had told his friends in College that it was his custom, as a rule, to read till midnight, and to go to bed quietly when he found himself too tired to absorb any more. He was not of an abstemious nature, although he was understood to be a professing Mohammedan; but he made no objection to attending the daily services in the College Chapel. His neighbours on his stair, both above, below, and opposite on the same floor, confirmed this. Not a sound had been heard in his rooms that night.

His tragic death had only become known that night because the night porter, before turning in to the Lodge, had gone the rounds, in accordance with the Dean's instructions, to look out for lights burning in rooms at that late hour. It was customary for undergraduates who kept lights going during the night to be called upon to account for the practice. The man had noticed that Pompoli's light was the only one on his stair burning that night, and had gone up to make enquiries. The door of the rooms was closed, though the oak was not sported. But, contrary to undergraduate custom, the door was locked. When no reply was vouchsafed to the series of loud knocks which he had given, and as no sound could be heard coming from within the room, Simpson, the night porter, became apprehensive and went to tell the Dean, who chanced to be still up in his rooms reading. When neither he nor the Dean had been able to secure any sort of answer to their repeated summonses, the Dean had given the order for the door to be forced.

There was a writing-table against the wall to the left of the door as one entered the room. One of the drawers in this was open, and the negro student was lying, huddled up, on his face, by the side of the chair drawn up at the table. His first impression had been that the student was drunk.

Further investigation revealed the tragic fact that the young man was dead, and that his body was already cold and stiff, and difficult to move for further inspection. He was in his day clothes, and the Dean had noticed a small round hole burned in the back of the light-coloured coat which he was wearing, just below the left shoulder-blade.

The Police Surgeon had subsequently discovered that death was due to a revolver-shot which had penetrated the heart, and he had succeeded in extracting the bullet that had caused the death, which must have been, according to the evidence the gunsmith gave later, fired from a small automatic revolver of a certain type.

Search had been made in the Cambridge police records, and no trace had been found of anyone in the town or University having applied, for years, for permission to carry a weapon of this type, and the lists of purchasers of small arms supplied by the various dealers in fire-arms in the town had yielded no more fruitful results.

It was small wonder that the Chief Constable and the Inspector were somewhat despondent about the possibility of tracing the murderer. Nor was there anything to show whether the crimes were the work of one person or two.

"It looks to me," said the Inspector at last, as he turned to open a few letters which had been delivered by the midday post, "as if there'll be a couple more murders to add to the list of unsolved crimes."

The Chief Constable smiled. He knew that if but one suspicion of a clue should chance to turn up, no man in his force would set off to follow it up more eagerly than Inspector Worplesdon. He had much to do in his own office, and rose to go. He had turned towards the door, when his companion gave an excited whistle. The Chief Constable turned again and saw that his subordinate was eagerly examining one of the letters which he had just opened from the pile which the orderly had placed in the basket beside him.

"What's the matter, Worplesdon?"

For reply the Inspector, whose face only a moment or two ago had been a picture of misery, was beaming hopefully.

"Something here—something that might help. Anonymous—but one never knows. Especially in this sort of case, mixed up with blacks and so on."

Chief Constable Deepcut was not impressed with the

Inspector's reasoning. But he waited to hear what there was to be told.

"Just a note—on a half-sheet of paper, as you see—with six words printed on it—in pretty cheap ink and with a bad pen."

"Well—what does it say?" asked Deepcut impatiently.

"'SUGGEST YOU SEARCH 54 PARK TERRACE,' that's all," said Worplesdon, handing the scrap to his superior.

"Look up the address then—quick," cried the Chief Constable.

The other rapidly turned the pages of the local directory which he had picked up from his desk. He found the place he wanted and then, throwing down the book in disgust, cried:

"A hoax—I thought so!"

"Why a hoax?" asked the Chief Constable, mystified.

"Fifty-four Park Terrace," said Worplesdon sarcastically, "is the address of Sir Wedgwood Camberley!"

CHAPTER VI

A FRUITLESS ENQUIRY

THE end of the term had come, the 'Varsity had gone down, and Cambridge, save for the daily streams of shoppers for the Christmas season who came into the town daily, whatever the weather, by bus and train from the country districts around, had settled down into its vacation capacity of an ordinary market town on the edge of the Fens.

The public, national and local, had lost interest in the two sensational murders of negro students which had ruffled the usual humdrum course of the Michaelmas Term, and as far as was known, the police, who had called in the services of Scotland Yard, had got no further with their researches into the mysterious crimes.

Scores of persons who might possibly have been expected to throw some light on the strange occurrences had been interviewed and their statements carefully taken down and tabulated, but it was clear that nothing very definite had emerged.

The task of the police in winnowing this material had been rendered the easier owing to the short time during which the two unfortunate undergraduates had been in England. They had but few contacts in the country, except within the confines of the University, and no sort of clue had emerged which pointed to any person, or persons, who could have borne so strong a grudge, or dislike, to them as to desire to take their lives.

The murderer, or murderers, had been very circumspect in choosing the times and places of the outrages. Trumpington

Street, round about midnight, is not a greatly frequented thoroughfare, and had the murderer of Ogu Kalawa been stalking his prey, as the wound in the back seemed to indicate, it would not have been difficult for him to screen himself from some chance passer-by amongst the trunks of the trees along Brookside lighted, as it was, by street lamps at pretty well-spaced intervals.

There was an equally small risk of detection, especially when no hint of the peril had been given, in the accomplishment and venue of the crime in Corpus Christi College, which had cost the life of the other West African victim, Karifu Pompoli. Members of other colleges, as well as its own, came frequently to visit friends in residence, and in the period after Hall was over there would be much coming and going of strangers as well as of members of Corpus.

The porter in the lodge would not be able to scrutinise the faces of everyone who came through the gates of the College, nor would such a practice normally be necessary. There were not more than half a dozen students with rooms on the African's stair, and it had been definitely established, during the course of the police enquiries, that between about 8 p.m. and 11.30 the only two who had been in their rooms all the time were the men who lived directly above and directly below the set occupied by Pompoli. There had been plenty of time for a stranger to wait his time until the stairway and the court were clear of visitors or residents and make his way up the staircase unobserved and unrecognised. The circumstances in which his body was found led the police to believe that the intruder had been someone known to the deceased, or someone, at least, with whom he was on not unfriendly terms. Pompoli appeared to have been shot in the back whilst he was bending down at his desk to secure something from one of the lower drawers.

Nothing had been found in any of the drawers which seemed to be of the least use in throwing light on the mysterious murder. Many of them were empty, and those which were not held mainly note-books—some partly filled with transcripts of the lectures which the young man had been attending—old pipes, boxes of matches and other odds and ends, such as one might expect to find in a student's possession.

In the actual drawer towards which the victim would appear to have been reaching, and which was partly opened when the police examined the room, there was nothing but a loose shilling and a torn and rather grimy envelope, which gave the appearance of having, at some time, been carried in the pocket of a coat. It was made of paper of a mauve shade, with a vivid purple inner lining, and there was a faint trace of some sort of perfume, or scent, still clinging to it when it was examined. It seemed more the kind of thing that one would have expected to find among the belongings of a woman, and doubtless had made its appeal to the negro student by reason of its bright colour and gay appearance.

On closer examination by the police it had been found to bear traces of finger-prints. Some of these had been compared with those of the dead man and had been discovered to correspond with them. But there were others, mostly blurred, which were those of someone else, and there was always the chance that, if any sort of clue chanced to make its appearance, they might be of use in piecing together the grim story which had preceded the tragedy.

The envelope was empty, but careful examination had revealed the presence of a short golden-coloured hair. Whether it had belonged to a man or a woman the experts had been unable to determine, and there was nothing to indicate how it had come to be there. The police had noted that there was a key in the keyhole of this particular drawer, and that all the other drawers of the desk were unlocked. The fair inference from this was that this particular drawer was the only one which the owner had kept habitually locked, and that, for some reason or other, he had opened it in connection with the visit of his assailant. This, too, was mere conjecture, for, as Inspector Worplesdon had pointed out, it might have been that the assailant had stolen softly into the room from the deserted stairway and surprised Pompoli as, for some reason or other, he happened to be opening the drawer.

The presence of the odd shilling might mean that this was the place where the African had kept his money: that the intruder had rifled it after killing his man, and overlooked the single coin which was left behind.

The negro student, who was the son of an African Chief, had been well supplied with money: his father's subjects knew that to their cost. When the time came round for the House Tax to be taken, the grasping old man levied, at the same time, a private tax of his own on such as had not the strength of mind to resist or refuse to pay the illegal impost, which more than equalled the amount demanded by the Government as a contribution towards the expense of keeping the Pax Britannica amongst its quarrelsome subjects. But no one had come forward who was able to say that Pompoli was in the habit of keeping large sums in cash about him.

Enquiries amongst the tradesmen in the town elicited the fact that the deceased was in debt to many of them for luxuries of one sort or another for which, when he had made use of them and the bills were presented, he had had no inclination to pay.

There was a tailor's bill running up to nearly thirty pounds: a chemist and perfumer had presented an account for a lengthy list of purchases including many bottles of one kind of patent medicine or another, and several expensive bottles of scent and bath salts. A grocer's bill, most of the items in which related to sweets, cakes, and sweet biscuits of costly brands ran well into two figures.

But though Cambridge tailors, chemists and grocers might have been excused for exhibiting a little impatience at the failure of their customer to settle his accounts promptly, they were not, so far as the police knew, in the habit of converting their feelings into homicidal tendencies and designs.

Several times during the course of the term Pompoli had obtained exeats from his tutor for the purpose of visiting London. He had stated that the object of his visits was an intention to visit a dentist, a tailor or a fellow-countryman in the capital, and he had given names and addresses to substantiate his claims.

The police had since attempted to verify these: but in one case, and in one case only, had they been successful. This was in connection with the dentist, a man practising in South Kensington, who was able, from his diary, to check one of the dates, when the negro had gone to town, as the occasion on which he had paid him a professional visit for the purpose of having one of his teeth extracted.

References to these enquiries had found their way into the Press, and had resulted in the coming forward of an undergraduate from King's named Farnham who, on the occasion of a birthday party in town at a big restaurant in the West End had testified to seeing the negro dining at the same place *à deux* with a pretty, made-up young woman, whose morals, he was inclined to think, were not above reproach.

This had suggested, for the time being, another line of attack on the problem. But though blackmail might have been suspected, it was difficult to reconcile murder and homicide with such a moral lapse on the part of the African student.

But the police had not yet ceased enquiries in directions suggested by the incident. It was on record that a student of Corpus, a second year man named Bramshot, who occupied rooms on Pompoli's stair opposite those of the African on the same landing, had occasionally dropped into the foreign "fresher's" rooms for a chat in the evening, and had recalled his disgust at some of the views which the other had expressed on the subject of women and their status. There had been arguments, which had frequently become heated, when the stranger had enlarged upon the subservient state of the other sex in his own country, and had expressed a certain guarded contempt for the men of white races who allowed their women-kind to occupy an honourable and respected place in society. He had, according to Bramshot's account, criticised European men for the way in which they had given in to their women's desire for freedom and equality.

That was all right so far as it went. Bramshot had read books on Africa: had realised that in the backward state of civilisation and education on the Coast, it was not unnatural that the newly-fledged Cambridge undergraduate should feel inclined to pour scorn and contempt on men who permitted their wives and daughters to share the privileges as well as the responsibilities of full citizenship. Africa, for the most part, was a couple of thousand years behind Europe. The so-called Chiefs, of whom Pompoli's father was one, were in reality nothing more than petty tribal heads, living in a state not far removed from that described in the patriarchal days of the Old Testament, when wives were chattels, at the mercy of their husbands who exercised complete power over their comings and goings, and ordered their whole lives in a fashion not far different from those of their sheep and cattle and other beasts of the field of which they were possessed.

The qualities most desirable in a woman, from Pompoli's point of view, were, first and foremost, an ability to bear strong, healthy children who should become assets to their father, if they were sons, to help him in the tilling of his lands and the governing of his chiefdom; if daughters, to bring grist to the family mill in the shape of handsome payment, in money and in kind, from prospective husbands. Nor was a wife's least desirable quality an ability to pander to the baser pleasures of her spouse, qualities which the negro, to the disgust of his listener who did not pretend to be unduly squeamish, would dilate upon in terms which nauseated his hearer.

Neither the Chief Constable of the Cambridge police, nor the London officers who had been sent to his assistance, had abandoned the possibility of there being a woman in the case, if only they could find her. But up to now there had been little sign that their researches in this direction were likely to be attended by success.

It looked, in fact, as though for the time being there must be a complete checkmate. All known facts had been sifted and collated, and there was just the possibility that, sooner or later, something might turn up, as much from luck as from any other cause, which would put their feet upon firmer ground. But there was no prophesying when, if ever, the *deus ex machina* would make his long-deferred appearance.

Ogu Kalawa's case was just as baffling. The police enquiries had not revealed the slightest possible motive in anyone in Cambridge, or elsewhere, for wishing to put an end to his life. He was a quieter, less blatant character than his compatriot, and there was no record of unpaid accounts for unnecessary and unsuitable luxuries. Nor was there any record, as there was in Pompoli's case, of his being mixed up with persons of the opposite sex of doubtful morality.

The only person in Cambridge with whom it could be said that he was not on the best of terms was his own fellow-countryman, the Corpus undergraduate. And as his own death seemed almost certainly to have occurred after that of Pompoli, this fact was of not much assistance towards the unravelling of the mystery. Even had there been definite proof the other way, and the guilt for the Corpus man's death laid certainly to the account of the young negro from St. John's, a fresh criminal had to be found as the murderer of Kalawa himself. The facts would not bear the possibility of a reversal. There was definite evidence that Pompoli had not left his rooms between the time the porter had seen him leave the lodge after posting the letter after Hall and the time when he was found dead in his own rooms.

It looked, as Chief Constable Deepcut was obliged to admit, that the double crime was to be added to the rapidly growing list of unsolved mysteries.

Only a few days were left before Christmas. The London men had returned to their own work a week since, with the promise that they would keep the matter fresh in their minds, and be ready to return to the University town the moment the Cambridge police could produce a reasonable excuse for their coming back to pursue their enquiries.

"It would be so much more satisfactory if we could at least start some definite line before the holidays. I feel," continued Inspector Worplesdon gloomily, "that my Christmas will be spoilt if I can't do something."

The Chief Constable, though younger than the Inspector, was of a more philosophical turn of mind.

"I shouldn't take it so much to heart if I were you," said he in an attempt to cheer his companion. "If the Yard too has to confess itself beaten—*for the time"*—he stressed the words—"there's nothing for *you* to be ashamed of. In police work as much as in any other—even more so perhaps—you can't make bricks without straw. Not much use inventing clues. We're not crime novelists—nor journalists either. For us it's *facts* and facts only that are of any use."

To the Chief Constable's surprise his colleague suddenly appeared to brighten.

"I tell you what," said he. "There *is* one fact that we haven't used. What about that anonymous note about the pistol—and the Professor?"

To the Inspector's disgust his chief burst out laughing.

"Why—you *don't* mean to say you're relying on that? I thought we both decided that that was just a joke. You *can't* be serious—or else you're very hard-up indeed—if you attach any importance to that. The freak of some undergraduate who wanted to have a lark—or to get his own back for something, the old fellow did to him in the past."

He laughed aloud again, and the Inspector, enraged, but unable to check his superior officer, went very red in the face.

"It may be only a straw—but that's what drowning men catch at. At any rate there can't be any harm in investigating."

"I wish you luck—if you're really going to tackle Sir Wedgwood—and on such an errand." He laughed again. "From what I've heard it would take a lion tamer to beard the Professor when he's roused. And he'll have some excuse for being roused if he comes to guess that you're suspecting him of murdering a nigger undergraduate!"

"All the same—he's not on the list of people who've got a licence for firearms. If he *has* got one—and it's quite easy, after all, to ask him—we've got a right to ask him what he's doing with it. You remember that one or two of the fellows we questioned mentioned an occasion, in Trinity Hall—the Hall of Trinity I should say—when the Professor wanted to eat this fellow Kalawa."

Worplesdon rose and put on his hat.

"Where are you off to now?" asked the Chief Constable in surprise.

"I'm going, sir," said he, "to fifty-four Park Terrace!"

CHAPTER VII

STALEMATE

Inspector Worplesdon felt less confident of himself as he drew nearer to Park Terrace. There was nothing about the day to raise his spirits. The drizzle of the earlier morning had settled into a steady downpour, and the mud from the wheels of the buses and cars plying through the wet and narrow streets was sprayed from time to time in generous jets over his trousers. At the moment when he had expressed to the Chief Constable his resolve to interview the Professor he had felt a certain amount of elation. The reasons which had led him to take the step had seemed far more cogent to him then than they did now that he had actually started on his way. Supposing the suspicions mentioned in the anonymous note had a foundation—supposing the Professor *had* got an automatic pistol—supposing he *had* neglected to report its possession to the Cambridge police, having made the actual purchase elsewhere? Professors were notoriously, proverbially absent-minded. He might, by chance, have committed a technical offence against the law, but that did not mean to say that he was in any way implicated in the two mysterious murders of negro students which had given rise to so much perplexity to him and to his staff. He had himself seen it stated in a local paper some time back that there was the possibility that the distinguished anthropologist might shortly be leaving for West Africa in connection with his work. It was customary, he believed, for persons going to that country, especially if their work was likely to take them into the wilder parts, to be adequately armed. The Cambridge police had had many applications from University students appointed to the Colonial Service for permits to hold small arms.

During the course of his investigation amongst undergraduates necessitated by the enquiries into the murders of Pompoli and Kalawa he had heard several times that Sir Wedgwood Camberley had a definite, if unreasonable bias, against coloured students, and against West African young men in particular. He had even heard of the incident in the Hall of Trinity College when Kalawa, in the morning of the day on which he had met his strange death in Trumpington Street, had incurred the wrath of the Professor by his late appearance at the lecture. But it seemed a little far-fetched, to say the least of it, to suppose that such irritation would be likely to engender homicidal tendencies in one of the most famous and distinguished teachers of whom Cambridge could boast.

Assuming this hypothesis, Sir Wedgwood must be a maniac. That sounded highly improbable, but it was not altogether to be ruled out. History, and the history of crime in particular, could show many instances of men of great distinction in many walks of life, who were as sane as anyone in the ordinary way, who had some peculiar kink in their brain which rendered them insane on some particular subject or with regard to some particular individual. There were, too, the idiosyncrasies noted by Shylock in the Merchant of Venice—the inexplicable aversion of certain individuals to cats—the strange effects produced in some by the music of the pipes.

His reflections in this strain cheered him a little. Perhaps he was not so far off the track as he had at first been inclined to fear. Perhaps Sir Wedgwood Camberley's aversion for the negro race was becoming a ruling passion. He had turned it over so much in his brain that he had become obsessed by it. The interruption of his lecture by the unfortunate young man from St. John's had just come at the critical moment and he had been unable to rest until he had purged his loathing for his whole race by stalking his prey that very night and removing him for ever from the chance of committing a similar offence.

He was drawing nearer and nearer to Park Terrace. The closer he approached his goal the less became his confidence in himself. The Chief Constable had hinted that the Professor was not an easy man to interview at any time. Supposing that his own suspicions were ill-founded and that the object of them had an inkling of the motive which had prompted this visit—he quailed at the thought of what might be the outcome of his morning's work. It might even cost him his job: might mean, at least, promotion downwards, relegation to some small country station where all hopes and future ambitions would be for ever buried, and he would drag out a monotonous, uneventful official existence until the time came for him to claim a meagre pension. Professor Camberley was a man of influence—he knew that both from the comments he had heard from the various undergraduates he had questioned, and from the references which were from time to time made about him in the national as well as in the local Press. If Sir Wedgwood, completely innocent of any sort of guilt in the matter on which he now proposed to see him, took umbrage at the suspicion which had been wrongly directed against him—and with next to no foundation—he might quite easily, by a word to those in authority in the police world, wreck for ever his chances of a successful career.

The Inspector had half a mind to turn back: the vision of a jejune future which his later thoughts had conjured up was not a pleasing one. He had, after all, very little on which to base his suspicions. The only reason, as he now realised, which had caused him to formulate the plan which he was now putting into execution was the complete absence elsewhere of any sort of real starting point for an enquiry.

He had come to the little pavilion behind the University Arms Hotel. Whether he decided to go on with his plan or not, it would do him no harm to give the matter a little more mature consideration. He turned aside from the terrace and sought the front of the little building. The benches were empty. The prospect of the Piece in front of him, in the pouring rain, was a melancholy one.

Closing his umbrella and shaking it out before him he sat down on one of the seats of the pavilion veranda and pulled out his cigarette case. Perhaps a quiet smoke would enable him to come to some definite conclusion and decide definitely whether or not it were worth the undoubted risks involved to carry out his intentions of interviewing the Professor of Experimental Anthropology. Grimly he smiled as he decided that he would not care merely to present a further subject for Sir Wedgwood's experiments in this direction.

He began to hope that the Professor might be out. But he hadn't much belief that this would prove to be the case. He had asked a constable to ring up the lecturer's house just before he started. The man had been put in touch with Sir Wedgwood, given a false name and a bogus message, and had been told, in no measured terms, what the Professor thought of a man who was so careless as to get the wrong number and disturb him when he was settled down to a busy morning's research work.

He realised that this was weakness. A distant church clock chimed eleven. It was highly unlikely that Sir Wedgwood, after the statement he had made to the constable, would be found anywhere that morning than in his own study. No—he had conceived the plan himself and he must go through with it. What would the Chief Constable say if he went back and reported that he had thought better of the matter and had gone back on his own tracks?

The cigarette soothed him: there was a break in the clouds, and for a few seconds the sun shone through and the rain fell with less intensity. So it was with police work. When everything seemed quite hopeless a faint spark of a clue would appear from nowhere and would grow in proportions until at length it became the hinge upon which the murderer's conviction hung. So far in the two cases which they were investigating there had been no clue at all—except that given by the anonymous note referring to the Professor. There was a certain amount of reason for supposing that Sir Wedgwood might at least in some way have something to say about the affair, even if he himself were not guilty. He was a negrophobe. One of the murdered men was a youth who had incurred the lecturer's displeasure on the day of his death. The other dead undergraduate, Pompoli, came from the same land as Kalawa, even though he did not happen to be one of the St. John's student's friends. It was possible that Sir Wedgwood, who was interested in the problem of the admission of coloured students to Cambridge, might know something of the contacts of the youths.

Inspector Worplesdon grunted as he lighted a fresh cigarette. He was trying to get himself away from the point at which he had started. When he set out that morning from the police station it had been with the definite idea of questioning Professor Camberley with a view to testing the theory as to whether he could by any chance be proved to be implicated in the crimes. And now here he was trying to make out to himself that his reason for the coming visit was of an entirely different nature. It was weakness. He had brought this thing upon himself—the Chief Constable had laughed at the idea as fantastic, but he must go through with it.

The quarter chimed and then the half-hour. A couple more cigarettes had been smoked. The rain was coming down faster than ever. It flashed through the Inspector's mind that his subconscious mind was seeking a loophole for the conscious. The later he put off his visit to 54 Park Terrace the better would be his chance of finding that Professor Camberley had gone out. He flung away a half smoked cigarette, and, putting up his umbrella, stepped out from under the pavilion veranda with an appearance of boldness which he was very far from feeling. In a few minutes—seconds even—he would be at Sir Wedgwood's door. Mechanically he opened the faded green gate which led into the small formal garden in front of the old house, and with an outward briskness of movement which was not a truthful reflection of his own inner thoughts, tugged at the old-fashioned iron bell-pull.

To his surprise the door was not opened by a maid, but by a pretty young girl whom he knew by sight as the Professor's own daughter. He blushed. This made things even a little more awkward than they were already. It was possible that Miss Camberley knew him too by sight, as he knew her.

"Is Sir Wedgwood Camberley at home?"

An expression of doubt seemed to flit across the face of the young girl. He was not in uniform but he could see that she recognised him as someone she had seen before. That would not be unexpected; he was a familiar figure in the town, but there was no special reason why she should know his calling.

"Ye-es." Dolly Camberley hesitated a little as she answered.

"Might I see him?"

"Dad's very busy this morning," said the girl wavering, still holding on to the front door and opening it no further.

This was a loophole for escape. Inspector Worplesdon was on the point of apologising and asking if he might call again at another time or day. He pulled himself together.

"I'm sorry, miss, to disturb him, but—but it's an important matter. I——"

"Oh—very well."

Dolly Camberley opened the door wider and stepped back to admit the visitor.

"I think—I think," she said hesitatingly, "that I've seen you before somewhere. But I can't quite remember who you are. I don't think you've ever been to see Daddy before?"

Inspector Worplesdon smiled uneasily as he stepped into the little hall.

"I'm often about the town, Miss Camberley. I'm—I'm——" he did not seem too anxious to disclose his identity. "I'm Inspector Worplesdon of the Cambridge police."

A look of recognition came into the girl's eyes, accompanied, so the Inspector thought, by a shade of alarm and anxiety.

"Oh, yes—of course: I think I saw you at the police sports in the summer. Won't you sit down while I go and tell Dad?"

She motioned him towards an uncomfortable looking antique wooden chair, cushionless and bare, which stood in a corner of the hall by a grandfather clock.

Inspector Worplesdon wavered again. If there were anything in his suspicions might not the girl warn her father and get him prepared for his visit? But he said nothing and took the seat which the girl had indicated.

"Very well, miss. I'll wait."

Dolly Camberley stepped across the hall to the door which led to her father's study. Knocking softly, she opened it, went in, and closed it behind her. Inspector Worplesdon's heart was beating rather faster than usual and he felt decidedly uncomfortable. He wished that he had made a little more preparation before undertaking this rather embarrassing visit. Through the closed door he could hear the loud voice of Sir Wedgwood in tones which sounded the reverse of amiable.

At last the suspense was over. The door of the study opened again, and Dolly Camberley stood upon the threshold.

"Dad says he'll see you."

She held the door open for the unwilling visitor, and as he entered and the girl made her quiet exit, Inspector Worplesdon felt more like a lion-tamer paying his first visit to the cage of a new purchase than anything else in the world.

"Good morning. What can I do for you?"

The Professor did not ask him to sit down. He did not attempt to rise from the chair at which he was sitting at his desk, and he regarded his visitor in no friendly manner over his right shoulder.

"Good morning, sir," said the Inspector, hiding his nervousness as best he could but without any surprising success.

Sir Wedgwood Camberley grunted and did not return the salutation.

"I'm extremely busy this morning and I've no idea to what I owe the pleasure of this visit. I presume you are something to do with the police?"

With each sentence that he spoke the Professor showed more irritation. He was not accustomed to speaking softly at any time, and the last few words were almost shouted.

Inspector Worplesdon decided that there was no use in employing finesse. If he tried to beat about the bush with a man of the Professor's temperament he would soon be completely at his mercy.

"I've reason to believe, sir, that you are in possession of fire-arms—of an automatic pistol, and that you either have no licence for this or have not reported the fact to the Cambridge police."

The change in Sir Wedgwood's manner was electrical. His ruddy complexion changed instantly to a deathly pallor, the arm which he had placed over the back of his chair as he turned to face his visitor fell limply to his side and his mouth, opened to reply to the Inspector, closed with a violent snap.

Inspector Worplesdon was as embarrassed as his host. He stood as if rooted to the ground, unable to say a word. The silence seemed to endure for an age, and before either man was able to break it, there was a soft tap on the door and Dolly Camberley came into the study without waiting for permission to enter.

"I'm sorry, Dad, to interrupt you, but I left something in one of your drawers last night—sorry I didn't tell you—and I want it now."

Without saying another word she went to the Professor's desk and pulled open the drawer from which she had seen her father take the automatic pistol the night after the murder of the two negro undergraduates.

Sir Wedgwood uttered no word. Inspector Worplesdon, taking advantage of the intrusion, stepped aside to let the girl pass and managed to obtain a full view of the drawer as she pulled it open.

"It's my watch: I was going to ask you to take it to London to be mended next time you went. But I've found a place here where they'll do it just as well."

As she spoke she drew from the drawer a small gold wrist watch which she took care to hold in such a way that the visitor should have every chance of verifying her words. The drawer was wide open, and the Inspector could see that, now that the watch was removed, it was entirely empty.

Sir Wedgwood Camberley bent over to look within the drawer. As he resumed his former position in his chair Inspector Worplesdon fancied that he heard him sigh a sigh of relief. He was completely mystified.

"Well, Inspector, now what can I do for you?"

The Professor now seemed quite collected, and his voice was as bland and polite as he could make it.

"I—I—that is—" stammered the nonplussed Worplesdon—"we got information that—well—what I told you, Sir. It must have been a hoax—a practical joke. I'm sorry."

He made the best excuses he could to the Professor and was politely escorted to the door by his daughter. But as he left the house he knew that the girl had outwitted him. There had been something in the desk drawer which neither the Professor nor Dolly Camberley wished him to see.

CHAPTER VIII

A ROUND TABLE CONFERENCE

THE Lent term had come round again, and with it the unfulfilled promise of Michaelmas had at last come to fruition. There had already been two days' skating on the frozen fens, and the frost looked like holding for some time more. Dolly Camberley in the dark blue woollen ski-ing suit which she had last used at the Winter Sports at Mürren the year before, looked the picture of glowing health as she poured out the tea for the two young men who were already launching a determined attack on the first plate of buttered muffins which the waitress at the King's Parade Restaurant had laid on the table a few moments before.

"Steady on, Pat! And you too, Geoffrey. Just like men to leave a girl to do all the work and gobble up all the food before I get a chance."

Geoffrey Cranston smiled good-humouredly.

"I apologise." But he made no attempt to restrain his attempts on the muffins.

"I don't," said Pat Frimley, unrepentant. "A little work won't do Dolly any harm. You're getting fat already: you've got nothing to do all day now that the Professor's off to Africa, and a little tea-pouring will do you a world of good."

"Hear, hear," echoed his friend, finishing off his first muffin and reaching for a second.

"Of all the *swine*—jolly good job you're both going to Africa too; manners don't matter in West Africa!"

"Oh," retorted Geoffrey Cranston, "and who told you that?"

"Yes, who?" queried Pat Frimley. "The only African you know, as far as I'm aware, is that poor fellow Kalawa who was done in last term by some blighter they haven't yet caught."

"And don't seem likely to catch either," said the other young man with a sneer. "It seems to me that when *we* get out there at the end of the year we'll look pretty damned foolish, going out to Africa to keep order in a country belonging to these black fellows when our own police—in Cambridge—can't even manage to make an arrest after two niggers have been done in—on the same night too!"

They were back on the old subject. The murder of the two unfortunate negro undergraduates had not remained a mere nine days' wonder. The University as a whole, as well as the police of the town, still felt decidedly sore on the matter. And criticism of the Force, by those who had not the slightest inkling of the difficulties with which its members had been faced, was harsh and unforgiving.

"I can't say," went on Geoffrey Cranston, "that I feel specially sorry for the fellow Pompoli. I know Bramshot of Corpus pretty well, and he's told me some pretty foul things about the chap. The way he used to go on about girls—white girls, I mean—was enough to make a man see red."

His tone grew indignant and Pat Frimley nodded agreement with his views.

"All the same—that's no excuse for murdering a chap in cold blood—just for *saying* things I mean—and none at all for the police who are supposed to find out who's guilty."

"That's true," said Frimley. "But in the case of Kalawa there's not even that to be said in extenuation. I knew the bloke—you'd met him too—and there was nothing at all like that about him."

Geoffrey Cranston nodded.

"I even introduced him once to you." He turned to Dolly Camberley.

"You did," said the girl, who had now finished her duties at the tea-pot and was beginning to appease the pangs of hunger which had been stimulated by an afternoon's hard skating on the fens. "And from what I saw of him I liked him: there wasn't anything to dislike. He was a good deal more polite too than some white men are—some, even, who aren't sitting a hundred miles from here!" She gave each of her companions a provocative glance. But the challenge was not accepted.

But Dolly Camberley had not finished.

"And even about Pompoli. I've read a good many books about Africa lately—novels and what not—and years ago, when I was quite a kid, I saw a film—*White Cargo* it was called. I was taken to it by an aunt—although it wasn't meant for children under sixteen—who thought, I suppose, that because there was 'white' in the title it would be all right for me."

She paused and scanned the faces of the two young men. It was clear that they, too, knew something of the picture, for there was a startled expression in the eyes of both Geoffrey and Pat as if they wondered what could be coming next. Dolly Camberley was always frank and outspoken and they were interested.

"What I mean to say—and you may be surprised, for it's not the conventional view, I know—is that I think that there are excuses even for Pompoli—even if what you've heard about him *is* true. I know we always talk as if white men could do just as they liked in West Africa—I mean as far as black women are concerned. But if the contrary happens, and black men come over here and try to be—well—a little too friendly with white women, there's no end of a dust-up."

Pat Frimley and Geoffrey Cranston looked at each other in quiet astonishment. This was a complete reversal of the orthodox attitude on the matter.

"I should say, speaking for myself, that there was more to be said for the blacks who went off the rails when they came over here than for the white men who do the same, with less excuse, when they get out to Africa."

"But——" put in Pat Frimley, in a vain attempt to turn the conversation into other channels.

"I haven't finished yet, Pat," said Dolly sweetly. "White men are always so kind and chivalrous to women. I'm sure you won't want to stop me before I've said what I want to?"

Pat Frimley gave up the attempt, and he and Geoffrey Cranston resigned themselves to listen. After all, they *were* hungry and the buttered muffins and hot tea were distinctly comforting after an afternoon on the ice, even if they did have to listen to a lot of wrong-headed preaching from a girl who, even if she had got some queer ideas, was decidedly pretty, amusing and generally desirable.

"Blacks—as Dad and you call them—come over here to get civilised: white men who go out to their country are *supposed* to be civilised already. If they both behave in the same way, and you think that the way is wrong, who's the more to blame—the white men who do wrong when they *know* they're doing wrong, or the black who don't see anything wrong in what they are doing, and don't know any better?"

"That's not the point," said Geoffrey Cranston, interrupting heatedly. "They've no business to come over here until they've learned to know better. They ought to learn a few things about our codes and morals and so on before they come here. We don't ask them to come to this country—and to Cambridge," he added rather lamely.

Pat Frimley smiled. Much as he agreed with his friend's point of view—though he had never troubled to think the matter out thoroughly—he appreciated the weakness of the argument.

Dolly Camberley, conscious of her dialectical success, went on unabashed.

"That's what Dad would say, of course: that's what he's always saying. 'We never asked them to come over here: why can't they stay in their own beastly country?' But it's all rather rot when you think it out. Couldn't they say just the same about us, and just as fairly? They never asked us to go and grab their country and put our own Colonies in it. We did it to keep other white men from coming along and doing the same, though now we try to pretend that we are doing it for the natives' own good."

"It's all very well, Dolly, for you to talk like that. But if you'd ever—well—come across one of these black fellows on the prowl——"

"I'd jolly well have known how to keep him off! You pointed Pompoli out to me one day at the pictures—sitting behind us. He didn't look any worse than—well—lots of people—and a good deal better than some."

The ferocity with which she spoke made both her listeners feel a certain amount of sympathy for the hypothetical black prowler.

"But there's something I rather want to talk to you about." Dolly Camberley dropped her voice and a more serious expression came over her features. She looked apprehensively about her; but though there were several other parties in the tea-shop, their members were all talking so loudly and with such animation that there was not much fear that they would overhear anything she might say.

"I dare say you heard that the police sent to interview Dad?"

Frimley and Cranston nodded. The matter had been suppressed in the local Press, but it had leaked out in town as well as in University circles that an Inspector had paid a professional visit to Professor Camberley. It had been rumoured that the matter concerned the possession of arms without a licence, and Sir Wedgwood's well-known views on the question of the sojourn of members of the coloured races in the University had naturally suggested the inference that the anthropologist might know something of one or the other of the mysterious murders of the two African students which had caused so great a sensation in Cambridge.

"Of course, *you* knew, Pat"—she turned to address Frimley—"that Dad *had* an automatic? I remember telling you."

Pat Frimley nodded.

"I remember. And I believe," he went on, flushing slightly, "that I mentioned the matter to you." He turned to Geoffrey Cranston.

"Yes—you did. But"—he added hastily, addressing the girl—"I can assure you that I never breathed a word of it to another living soul."

Dolly Camberley laughed.

"I don't expect you did. I never told Pat that he need not tell anyone. He's got lots of discretion, bless him, though he is such a babe in some ways, and I'm quite sure that if he did choose to tell anyone he'd not do so unless he felt he could trust them."

Geoffrey Cranston seemed relieved at this sally. He gave a bow of mock gratitude. He was just about to speak, when Dolly continued.

"What I didn't tell you," she turned again to Pat Frimley, "and you mustn't—either of you—breathe a word of it to anyone else until I give you permission—was that father *was* out that night, and that he must have passed by where Mr. Kalawa was found dead—in Brookside—more or less about the time that the murder took place."

Pat Frimley and Geoffrey Cranston looked at each other in astonishment. They hastened to assure the girl that the secret was as safe in their keeping as in her own.

"I know—I know. That's why I told you. It's possible—in case the police make any silly fuss—that I may want your help."

Both emphatically asserted their loyalty to Dolly Camberley and her father.

"It really was most extraordinary." She still talked in low tones to avoid any possibility of her words being overheard by persons sitting at neighbouring tables, and Pat Frimley and Geoffrey Cranston had to lean well forward so as to be able to catch her meaning. The younger of the two, Frimley, found nothing distasteful in the necessity which compelled him to place his own head in close proximity to that of the pretty young daughter of the Professor whose physical attractions, as he began to realise, were as worthy of his admiration as was the spirit which she showed in her defence of Sir Wedgwood Camberley.

"Dad had been out to visit a friend—Professor Horsell of St. John's—who lives out a little way down Trumpington Road. He told me this after the Inspector had called to enquire about the revolver. He said that he was passing the Leys School—near the pillar-box in the wall as far as he could remember—on the night when the two murders happened. He did see some people about on the other side of the road, near Brookside, and had some faint recollection of what sounded like a shot and then a splash and a sound like somebody falling into water. But you know Dad—he's very absent-minded—or rather—always thinking over some problem in his own mind, and he didn't pay any attention to it and didn't even remember it till we heard about the murders next morning. He said if he thought anything about it at all that it might be some undergraduate who had had too much to drink having a squabble with somebody and falling into the water. Anyway, it was no business of his and he wouldn't have dreamed of trying to interfere. When he found out that it was a murder that had happened, and he knew that he must have been near the scene of it, he was a bit upset. Especially when he knew that it had been committed with a small automatic of the kind that he had himself. To make things worse for him, the man who was murdered was an *African* undergraduate, and his views about black men in the University were so well known, and he had expressed them so often, that he began to be nervous that his own name might be connected with the crime. Of course, I told him that all this was absurd, and that no one would dream of thinking anything of the kind. But Dad is very obstinate, and also—though you mightn't think so unless you knew him very well—very nervous and timid about some things."

This piece of information was news to both the girl's hearers, and they found it difficult to repress a smile. They remembered stories which appeared occasionally in comic papers which dealt with the reactions of lion-tamers when they had to deal with their own wives instead of with the feline creatures with whom they had to deal in the course of their profession and applied the analogy to the case of the Cambridge Professor of Experimental Anthropology.

"When I found him, the night after the murders, in his study with the revolver in his hand, he admitted afterwards that he had not taken the trouble to inform the local police, as he thought he ought to have done, when he bought the revolver in London and brought it here when he expected to start for his African trip.

Although he did not exactly expect a visit from the police, he realised that things might prove a bit awkward for him if it came out later that he had the thing irregularly, and that it was found that he, whose prejudices against coloured undergraduates in Cambridge—in England in fact—were known to be so strong—was actually near one of the men at the time that he was murdered, and that no arrest had been made. When I surprised him in his study with the pistol the night after the murder he had been cleaning it before hiding it away. He had, one day when I was out, fired a few practice shots in the garden. He thought that, in case the weapon did come to be found, the fact that it had dirty barrels would make things all the more serious for him. To cut a long story short, I knew it was of no use asking Dad to let me have charge of the thing. He insisted in keeping it in his drawer. But I found a key that fitted it, and one day, when he was out, in case of complications, unlocked the desk and took out the pistol and hid it away in my own room. It was lucky I did so, for I saw that when the Inspector called Dad was in an awful stew. He thought the man might have power to search his room for the unlicensed pistol. So when he was interviewing Mr. Worplesdon in his study I went in and opened the drawer in front of the policeman and brought out my watch which I had put there in place of the revolver!"

Dolly's hearers were amused at the story; but they found it rather difficult to believe the Professor's perturbation, unless, indeed, he actually did secretly know something about the murder or murders which he did not wish to come out in public. But neither of the young men chose to voice his suspicions. Pat Frimley was continually being more and more impressed with the desirability of his daughter, and her known loyalty to her father would have effectually put an end to his hopes in her direction had he dared to make a suggestion that Sir Wedgwood might be in any way implicated.

Geoffrey Cranston was heart-whole, for the present. But good taste and a genuine desire for the girl's continued friendship prevented him also from pursuing a dangerous subject.

The three had finished their tea and as Pat Frimley smoked his pipe and the girl and Geoffrey Cranston their cigarettes they continued to explore other aspects of the topic which still held general interest in the University town.

"I've read everything, I think, that's been printed about these affairs," said Frimley judicially, "and there's just one thing that strikes me and makes me think that the police may be barking up the wrong tree all the time. You'll remember that, at the inquest, the policeman, King, who came along after the two chaps had discovered Kalawa's body, definitely said something about another black fellow being in the little crowd that gathered in Brookside?"

Cranston and the girl nodded.

"Well," went on Frimley, weighing his words as if to impress his audience, "I can't help thinking that that was a point that ought to have been gone into. As far as we know, no attempt was ever made to trace this chap; and, though the place is getting blacker than ever every term, there still *are* a few more whites than blacks in the 'Varsity, and it shouldn't have been—shouldn't be now—too hard to trace the fellow and get his story—for what it's worth."

"I agree," said Geoffrey Cranston. "With all their enquiries they haven't found out any white man who would have a real reason for wanting to do in either of these blacks. But they're a quarrel-some lot, according to what we've been told in lectures and things, amongst themselves, and I don't see why the explanation mayn't be traced back to some feud or other way out in West Africa itself."

"Our Geoffrey's getting quite brilliant," exclaimed Dolly Camberley. "I think you'd better change your plans. Instead of going out to West Africa why not get a job with the C.I.D." Then her tone changed suddenly. "But—seriously—I think there may be something in what you say. But how can we be sure that the police haven't already followed up this line on the quiet?"

Geoffrey Cranston shook his head.

"*Somebody* in *some* college would have been bound to hear something about it. There seems precious little that the police have done so far in Cambridge about this business that hasn't got into the papers—the London as well as the local. Besides, I don't quite see why they should necessarily have thought of this line at all. It would only be as a sort of last resource. And I suppose they think they haven't come to that yet. Perhaps they've got reasons for thinking so that we know nothing about."

Pat Frimley had been pulling thoughtfully at his pipe for some time.

"Well, Geoffrey, what about our doing a little sleuthing on our own? After all, as we are actually going out to the Coast, the matter concerns us as much as anyone else. We—that is I—shall feel in a sort of false position—going out there to show the blacks how to do things when, in a matter that's so important to them, we haven't been able to do a thing ourselves."

"Well done, Pat," cried Dolly Camberley. She was pleased at the spirit shown by the young man. There was still, she felt, some sort of a cloud hanging over her father in connection with the murders. Not that she for one moment believed that he had been in any way implicated, but she knew what rumour was, especially in the University town, and she would have welcomed an explanation of the matter which would completely clear Sir Wedgwood in the eyes of the public, and in the minds of the local gossips. She did not doubt that rumours of the Inspector's visit were on their rounds, and she would have liked to have been able effectively to silence them. "I don't suppose the police will thank you—they're always so sure of themselves—but I don't think we need bother our heads about that."

"There's no need for the police," said Frimley, "to know anything whatever about it—until we choose to tell them. I suppose, as a matter of policy, we ought just to mention our ideas and suspicions to them, otherwise they might get the idea that we were interested—in the wrong way."

Geoffrey Cranston nodded.

"That's true," he said. And Dolly Camberley agreed.

"It oughtn't," said Frimley, "to be very difficult to trace the black fellow who was out that night—at the scene of the first murder—

at the very time that it happened; and if we can manage to discover the chap's name we can either inform the police at once, for anything they care to do, or make a few enquiries about him ourselves. And I've got a sort of hunch that these two affairs were somehow or other mixed up together, and that if we can find out anything really definite about *one* of them we shan't be very far off clearing up the other two."

The other two members of the party agreed with him heartily and the proposal was carried with acclamation.

"And here," said Geoffrey Cranston, raising his empty tea-cup with mock gravity and a somewhat cynical smile, "is to the health of the Cambridge Amateur Detective Society—though it might be as well not to get ourselves known by its initials!"

CHAPTER IX

AN AFRICAN IDYLL

If Professor Camberley didn't like Africans, he had come very soon to the conclusion that he liked their country even less. From the day that he had landed at the port of Old Guinea, Edwardsville, on the West Coast, he had regretted his decision to accept the offer of the University to subsidise his tour in the Black Continent to provide him with means of actual research on the spot and a chance of first-hand study of its anthropological data.

In fact, his loathing for the Coast and all that it implied dated further back than the actual date of his embarkation, for he found nothing congenial in the company on board the smart new motor liner which had brought him out on his tour of inspection, and no means of satisfying his own scholarly tastes.

If there was one thing in the world which roused his contempt and scorn more than another it was the idea of a fancy dress dance. He always said that the human race looked quite ridiculous enough in its normal civilised state without the necessity of making itself still more ridiculous by getting itself up to look like all sorts of things that it had no honest pretensions to be. There were those, in Cambridge and elsewhere, who hinted that if all the human race had looked like Sir Wedgwood Camberley, the worst-dressed and untidiest man amongst a set of men who were remarkable neither for their dress nor for their neatness, there would have been something to be said for his contentions.

He had frowned upon the modern habit of the undergraduate

of taking morning sherry and attending occasional cocktail parties: but on the Coast-bound boat there were those who began the day with beer for breakfast, continued it with cocktails, whiskies and sodas, gins and bitters and concoctions of various kinds of liquors whenever the bar was open until the time it closed at night, when they solaced themselves for the deprivation of its facilities for the slaking of their thirst by taking a bottle of whisky to their cabins with them.

Cards were anathema to the Professor; but there were those aboard in plenty who monopolised the best tables in the lounge and smoke-room from immediately after breakfast until they finally turned m at night. And judging from the conversations which he overheard through the none too thick walls of his cabin, they gave rein to the ruling passion until the moment they fell asleep.

Sir Wedgwood had heard of sweepstakes; but he had not really gathered their true nature until he boarded the West African liner. On shipboard the organising and running of this foolish lottery on the ship's twenty-four hour run took up the whole of the morning of those who were not playing bridge or indulging in frivolous and stupid conversations from their chairs on the deck with companions of the opposite sex to their own.

He did manage to find one serious-minded person on board, an American missionary who had apparently found that there was so little evangelising work to do in his own highly Christian country that he was going to West Africa to try his 'prentice hand on the clamouring heathen there. But even here there was a fly in the ointment: for on the third day out Sir Wedgwood had discovered that the Rev. Septimus P. Johnson was a fundamentalist from Dayton, Ohio, whose views on evolution were scarcely calculated to impress a man who had made a life-long study of scientific anthropology.

Looking back on a life which had lasted for nearly sixty years, Sir Wedgwood Camberley found it difficult to recall ten consecutive days on which he had felt so thoroughly bored and out of tune with his surroundings. Even Africa, to which he by no means looked forward, would be something of a relief from this.

He had, as it were, been translated to another world, a world where the words of even the most eminent professors, dilating upon their own especial subjects, were listened to with bored politeness and, on occasions, with a boredom which was not even polite.

He had heard visitors "doing" Cambridge say to their guides, professional or otherwise, when he passed: "Who is that distinguished looking man with the fine head?" and had been conscious of a reverential awe in their voices when they had been informed. It was otherwise on the African liner. One day, as he sat in his deck-chair, just outside the smoking-room after lunch, trying to collect his thoughts over a German scientist's monograph on "Diet in Relation to Race" he had heard a slightly inebriated trader, the sight of whom he detested, ask a young Government officer, whose potations had been no less deep than his own "who the ugly beggar (only he used another word) was with the second-hand bags and the walrus moustache." He had also heard the other's reply to the effect that "it was only some old fossil going out to find out how many brands of bugs and fleas there were on the Coast that you didn't find at home—as if there weren't enough already!"

There had been compensations when he landed and stayed a couple of nights with the Governor at the Residency. The Governor was an Oxford man, and had certainly heard of Sir Wedgwood even before he had received a despatch from the Colonial Office announcing his coming; but even he showed a lamentable ignorance of the work of an experimental anthropologist and had bored the Professor by trying to remember passages of Homer and Vergil of which fifty per cent of the words in each line had escaped his memory. Sir Wedgwood Camberley had never been a classical scholar, and had had the greatest difficulty in satisfying the examiners in the subject in his "Little Go."

There was, however, some pretension to civilisation in His Excellency's *ménage* and Sir Wedgwood had recovered slightly the spirits which had been somewhat damped on the trying outward voyage. But he found difficulty in sleeping owing to the heat and the stuffiness of the air under a mosquito net, together with the everlasting noises of the crickets in the garden.

He had hoped that his aversion to the negro race would perhaps be mitigated when he came upon them in their own land: he supposed that his dislike for them might be the outcome of his resentment at their aping the white man in his own country. But it did not take him long to come to the conclusion that it was the black skin *per se* which was the subject of his dislike. His distaste for the Africans was not mitigated by the difficulty with which he made himself understood by the servants and clerks with whom he came in contact. Even if they didn't actually talk the pidgin English which is the lingua franca of the Coast, they spoke with such strange accents and intonations that he could scarcely understand a word they addressed to him without the aid of an interpreter.

But Sir Wedgwood was not the man to turn back once he had set his hand to the plough. He had arranged to spend three months in the Colony, and he determined to go through with his full programme. He had been advised by those who knew the country that he would be able to find little that would be of value to him amongst the semi-sophisticated natives of the Coast towns, and the Governor had arranged for him to tour the Central Province, where he, under the auspices and protection of the various District Commissioners could study language, music, customs and the shapes of the heads of his subjects to his heart's content, undisturbed by having to observe the conventions of official Coast life.

"And whilst you're up there," the Governor said, "you'll probably come across the fathers of both Kalawa and Pompoli, the young men who were so unfortunately murdered in Cambridge. They're both Chiefs, in their own right, and if the Provincial Commissioner's reports are correct, there's no love lost between them."

Sir Wedgwood Camberley surveyed with disgust the sleeping quarters in the hut which was assigned to him by the young District

Commissioner who had welcomed him at the chief station of the Province in the absence of the Provincial Commissioner on tour in some distant part of his territory. He too proved to be an Oxonian, and a classic, and had displayed no particular interest in the Professor's mission. His bearing had been courteous enough; but Sir Wedgwood felt that he was acting under orders in providing for the needs of the distinguished visitor to his Province, and had no deep convictions as to the use which he was doing or professing to do for mankind.

"If, sir, you'd prefer to have your own quarters—and I daresay you will have a lot of work to do and will want to be quiet and undisturbed—I have prepared the Rest House for you, and I think you'll be comfortable, as comfortable, that is, as anyone *can* be in this bl——," then he remembered to whom he was talking, "blessed country."

He had arrived late in the evening, after a hot and dusty tramp, partly on foot and partly in a hammock carried on the heads of four native "boys," from the railway station at Mandu, and had accepted the hospitality of his young host with gratitude. The District Commissioner's bungalow—a recent concrete and wood building on high cement pillars—was comfortable enough with its polished floors, reed mats, and Indian curtains, and he had even enjoyed the meal.

If only the Rest House of which young Woodward spoke were similar to the District Commissioner's own quarters, he felt that he would be able to endure his stay in Africa with a certain amount of equanimity.

"All your loads are there—and I expect your cook and houseboy—if they were recommended to you by H.E.—will have got everything ready, and you will be able to turn in and have a good night's rest."

Sir Wedgwood Camberley nodded. He had not had time to change for the meal with his host, and was still in the khaki trousers and black alpaca coat in which he had made his tiring journey. He felt that the coffee and liqueur with which the District Commissioner regaled him were a little incongruous with such attire. But the Benedictine was comforting—he had refused any other kind of alcohol before or during dinner—and he did not refuse when Woodward offered him a second. The station was built on a small, flat-topped hill rising out of grass plain country, and as he lay back in a deck chair on the veranda he could see, in the bright light of a rising moon, a dark patch in the whiteness of the land under the moonshine, which Woodward told him was a native village. The sound of wild drumming rose spasmodically from time to time in the still air, and the Professor felt a creepy feeling down his spine. Was this preparation for a native war—a massacre, perhaps, of the District Commissioner and any whites in his Province? Even as he was musing upon this, his host broke the silence.

"It's a funny thing," he said. "That village isn't in his country—but Chief Brima Kafari—the father of one of those two poor chaps who was murdered in Cambridge last year—Pompoli, I think it was, is there to-night. Says he wants to see me in the morning, but he hasn't told me what it's about."

The Rest House had turned out to be just a mud shack—a fairly big mud shack—with two rooms—a space between—and a wide encircling veranda—the whole roofed in with a thick thatch of dried grass. Sir Wedgwood was distinctly ill at ease. He couldn't very well go back on his words and send over and ask his host whether he could sleep at his securer house for the night. Yet the sight of the camp-bed, with its curtain, set up on a ground-sheet in one of the small, mud-walled, whitewashed rooms of the Rest House, a camp-chair and folding wash-basin beside it, did not inspire him. His servants, without asking permission, had departed before he arrived back from the District Commissioner's house after dinner, and his sole companion was the native policeman who had been detailed as his orderly by his host.

At last, having ordered the man to keep watch for the night on the veranda outside, he undressed and got into the narrow bed. The sound of the native drums still beat upon his ears. The rhythm seemed to be faster—the eerie note more menacing than it had been before. He remembered what Woodward had said about the Chief who was staying in the neighbouring village that night. Suspicion, he knew, had been cast upon him, ridiculously enough, in the matter of the Cambridge murders. What if—what if—Brima Kafari had vowed vengeance upon the killer of his son?

CHAPTER X

EXPERIMENTAL ANTHROPOLOGY

IT was with some difficulty that Professor Camberley managed to get to sleep that night. He could not keep his mind off the menacing sound of those tomtoms away in the native village down the hill. Yet he did not care to send a note over to his young host to disclose his suspicions as to their significance. He might, after all, be making a complete fool of himself. Was it likely that a West African district, hitherto peaceful, should suddenly burst into insurrection just because he happened to visit it? Probably the Chief, if his arrival had anything to do with the tragedy which had ended his son's life at Cambridge at all, just wanted to hear all that was to be known from a white man who actually lived in the town.

After a restless night Sir Wedgwood woke early, and began to wish that he had never undertaken this expedition at all. There was no real need for a scientist in his particular branch of science to visit the actual country which was the home of the peoples he had set himself out to study. There were plenty of skulls and bones in the museum at Cambridge, and elsewhere, from which he could deduce all that he needed to know, and very complete collections of the clothing, utensils, and implements of various kinds which the natives used and which were all of the utmost value in the study of their racial characteristics. He had been foolish to allow himself to be persuaded against his own inclinations and convictions.

He realised, however, that there was not much point in raising these objections now. He was actually in West Africa, in the bush at that, and he must go through with it, remain for the allotted three months and make the best of it. It was quite possible that, after he had got accustomed to the strange life to which he had been introduced, he would change his mind.

The day was dawning: he could see the cold grey light creeping through the rough wooden window of the whitewashed mud room in which his camp-bed had been set up. There was no sign of life stirring anywhere, yet he was restless and felt that, tired though he was after his troubled night, he could not go to sleep again. He pulled up the side of his mosquito curtain and with a certain amount of difficulty, managed to drag his limbs on to the floor and get out of the bed. As his foot touched the canvas groundsheet which his servant had spread out to prevent his soiling his socks on the rough mud floor, he gave a slight scream of terror. His foot had come into contact with something cold and clammy. A snake! How foolish he had been not to look to make sure before he attempted to get up. His heart beat violently and he scarcely dared to look. In the scanty light he was able to discern a squat, unshapely mass hopping away in an ungainly manner. It was only a frog or a toad after all.

To his dismay he next found that the folds of his mosquito curtain were wringing wet—no doubt with the damp, cold mist which was billowing in through the ever-lightening window space. His pyjamas, too, were uncomfortably moist, and he began to have visions of being laid up with a go of rheumatic fever. Malaria, at the least, for he had read that the malarial germs were ever present in the blood of Europeans who had the temerity to face the treachery of the West African climate, and that there was nothing like humidity to lure them forth to do their worst.

He felt thoroughly miserable, and he was aware of a painful spot on his left shoulder-blade. He began to imagine all kinds of causes for this phenomenon, when, his eye falling for a moment on the bed from which he had emerged, he noted that the reason for it was the slipping from beneath his pillow of his automatic pistol, the very one which had been the cause of the Police Inspector's visit to him at Park Terrace.

He wondered, as he mused upon his troubles, at the rapidity with which the African dawn was breaking. He could hear the sound of chattering and twittering birds in the clumps of banana plants which surrounded the little compound of the mud Rest House, and as the day grew brighter and brighter, the mist began to lift and the first rays of the sun illumined the edge of the small coppice which faced the window from which he looked out.

He looked at his watch. It was six o'clock, but there was no sign of any of his domestic staff. This irritated him, for he felt the need of a warm drink of tea to drive away some of the chill which the damp night had engendered in his bones. He would make some himself. He looked round the bedroom. There was nothing there to assist him in his scheme. He knew, from what his host had told him the night before that the kitchen was a small mud hut placed at some distance from the main building, with no sort of range or stove. The native cooks and servants performed such feats as cooking meals and heating bath water over a few burning sticks placed in the shape of a star, their lighted points towards the centre, and pushed them inwards from time to time as the kindling was consumed. He began to wish that something of a practical nature had been included in his early curriculum. A knowledge of men's skulls, and the sort of brains that they contained, and the study of what they ate and how they ate and cooked it, was all very well. But Sir Wedgwood Camberley at the present moment would have given all his amassed knowledge on the subject for a cup of hot tea, if only he had known how to make it.

He went out on to the veranda, which faced out over the brow of the hill which overhung the village from which the sounds of the tomtoms had come the night before. For a moment or two he was puzzled by an untidy bundle, as it seemed, wrapped up in a brown blanket, sprawling on a couple of native mats across the entrance. He was still more startled when the mass began to move and revealed itself as the police orderly who had watched over his own slumbers. When the apparition realised that it was in the presence of its temporary white master, it unfolded itself with alacrity and, shaking off the blanket and donning fez and belt, got up and gave a sleepy salute.

Sir Wedgwood Camberley had a bright idea. As the servants had not yet put in an appearance, he would make use of the Government orderly. His host had already sung the praises of his Force, the members of which appeared to be capable of doing any conceivable job that happened to be wanted in the bush, from cutting their master's hair to making a swizzle-stick for cocktails.

"Good morning, my man." The Professor tried to infuse a little dignity into his tones: but he felt that the effort was not very successful. He felt considerably less dignified in his present attire of pyjamas, a Terry towelling dressing-gown and gum boots than he was accustomed to feel swathed in an academic gown, as he lectured to large classes of undergraduates in the Hall of Trinity at Cambridge.

"Morning, sah," replied the constable, a little sheepishly and divining from his temporary master's mode of address that he was scarcely likely to understand him when he ventured on to conversation at large.

"The servants—ah—have not yet put in an appearance. Do you think *you* could make me a cup of tea?"

The orderly scratched his head but did not reply. He did not wish to commit himself to explaining that he had not understood the request.

Sir Wedgwood Camberley regretted that he had not made a note of where the cook kept his gear. Had he been able to point to a kettle and a teapot there would have been little need for him to speak at all.

Still, he felt that he must make the effort. He longed for a cup of tea to refresh himself, and wished more than ever that he had never allowed himself to be persuaded to leave his own comfortable quarters in Park Terrace where he was so efficiently managed and looked after by his capable daughter.

"I'm thirsty," he said, coming down to essentials. "I want to drink."

The orderly's face brightened up. He now appeared to understand what it was that Sir Wedgwood wanted. Straightening his cap and giving a fresh hitch to his belt he saluted again, considerably more smartly than before, and went into the second room of the mud Rest House, the living-room as the District Commissioner had called it; though Sir Wedgwood had made a mental note at the time that he would sooner be dead once and for all than have to dwell in such an apartment.

During the man's absence the Professor sat down in a canvas chair on the mud veranda and looked out into the compound which reached as far as the precipitous slopes of the hill on which the Government station was situated and at the foot of which nestled the village where, as he understood, Chief Brima Kafari, father of the dead undergraduate Pompoli, had spent the night before his visit to the District Commissioner.

It was foolish, he felt, to worry about the matter. But he could not help reverting to Woodward's words of the evening before, and to wonder whether the Chief's visit had any connection with his own presence at Mandu, and whether it was due to the fact of his own connection with the town in which his unfortunate son had come by his mysterious death. It was foolish, of course, he realised, to indulge in such speculations. Even if they chanced to be true, there was nothing he had to fear himself. He had had no kind of responsibility in connection with the young man's death: he was not even a Proctor; and he did not see how, even if he were, he could be held culpable in connection with the ghastly crime. It was true that there had been silly rumours flying about, owing to his supposed possession of an automatic pistol of the same kind as that which had caused the death of Pompoli of Corpus. It was also conceivable that, through correspondence with other West Africans resident in England, the Chief had heard something about that incident. But it was carrying things rather far to presume that because of that small isolated fact, details of which had not even percolated to the local Press, Chief Brima Kafari had paid a special visit to Mandu, from his own village over a hundred miles away, on the chance either of hearing more of his son's end or of attempting to fix the responsibility upon him.

When he passed these thoughts in review for the second time in his mind he began to wonder whether he were not becoming a little unhinged in mind. The more he turned the matter over the more ridiculous did his fears seem to him.

He could hear the orderly fumbling about in the room behind him. But after what Woodward had told him of the intelligence and capabilities of the members of his police force, he decided not to disturb him: it would probably only delay the preparation of the cup of tea for which he was longing.

He had often heard stories of the strange atmosphere of Africa, and especially of West Africa, and of its curious effect on the minds of Europeans who visited it. And he began already to believe that there was something in it. The strangeness of his surroundings, unlike anything he had ever seen or thought of before, coupled with the restlessness which was natural for one spending his first night in a camp bed in a Rest House which at home would have been considered rather inferior quarters for prize—or even ordinary—pigs, had acted upon his nerves and brought on a kind of mild mental hysteria.

It would make an interesting subject for a monograph in connection with his special branch of study: the effect of a barbaric setting upon the mind of civilised Aryans. How that effect might be translated from thought into action, and how, as its effect, civilisation might be engulfed anew by barbarism.

As the sun rose higher in the heavens, and the twitterings and songs of a thousand unfamiliar birds began to beat upon his ears from every quarter, he began to forget his worries and dark thoughts and to wonder at the wild beauty of the land which was being revealed before him.

For miles in front of him there seemed to be an expanse of undulating plain, broken here and there by the sudden rising of a quaint, square-topped low hill, whose sides were clad with masses of dark green vegetation. He could see nothing that could be identified in the European sense as a town or village, but here and there, from amidst clumps of trees and bushes, there were to be seen spirals of blue smoke—wood smoke—winding up into the still air to mark the place of human habitations. The secret of the invisibility of the native townships was explained, so the Professor guessed, by the fact that they consisted of low mud huts with thatched roofs, like that of the Rest House in which he was himself lodged, which would, in the far distance, blend perfectly with the natural colours of the far-flung landscape which stretched out before him.

His thoughts were interrupted by the reappearance of the constable from the room behind him, bearing a metal tray on which were set out on a somewhat grimy dish-cloth, intended to do duty for a doily, a sparklet bottle, a large tumbler, and a full bottle of whisky from which the cork had only just been extracted.

Before Sir Wedgwood could utter a word, the orderly, saluting with his free hand, had placed the tray on a wicker table beside his master's chair and held the whisky bottle at an angle to the tumbler, inviting the Professor to "say when."

For the moment he was too amazed to speak. Before he could do so, there was the sound of booted feet on the gravel path which led from the back part of the compound to the front of the Rest House.

The sound was quickly followed by the appearance of young Woodward, the District Commissioner, looking fresh and spruce in a clean bush shirt with a dark red silk tie—the colour of the Colony—khaki shorts and spotless grey stockings. He held his helmet in his hand, for the sun was not high enough yet to be dangerous.

"Good morning, sir."

Sir Wedgwood felt for the moment like a small child detected in the act of stealing jam from a forbidden cupboard. He remembered some sententious remarks which he had delivered at dinner with his host the night before about the deleterious effect of strong liquor on those who made a habit of indulging in it to excess on the "Coast." And here he was, caught apparently by his young host in the act of having a whisky and soda before breakfast!

He was too astonished for the time being to make any coherent utterance, and the brusque way in which he forced up the hand of the obliging constable holding the bottle over the tumbler might have been interpreted in more ways than one.

"Good morning, sir."

That was all Woodward said; though the Professor, aware of the compromising look of the situation in which the man's stupidity had placed him, thought that he detected the suspicion of a smile in his eyes.

He felt that, in every way, he was caught at a disadvantage. He replied, as politely as he could, to his early visitor, and began at once to explain away the incident.

Young Woodward laughed heartily.

"It's a queer country, sir," said the District Commissioner, taking a seat on the veranda and trying to put his distinguished visitor at ease. "If you knew whose orderly this man had been for several years, not so very long ago, you wouldn't be surprised. The only words you spoke that he understood were 'drink' and 'thirsty.' His previous master died in the Edwardsville Nursing Home here of delirium tremens. Now, perhaps, you will understand the thing better."

So the incident was passed off with a laugh.

"But there was something that I had to tell you." The District Commissioner's tones, as he pulled rather nervously at his cigarette, grew more serious. "I know you haven't very much time in the country, and that you have a lot to get through." He glanced at the piles of packing-cases which were stacked in the far corner of the Rest House veranda. "I believe that you want to study the natives as closely as possible—take measurements—get records of their songs and speech—and all that."

Sir Wedgwood nodded. He had told the young man the night before some of the things which he had hoped to accomplish.

"If you want to do all that, of course I can help you. The Governor has told me to do everything I can to make things as easy as possible for you. But—and this is the point: on the surface, the people who matter out here are the Government officers, like myself. And so we are—up to a point. We've got to see that the laws are kept and all that. But really, to get down to bedrock, when all's said and done, the people who really rule the country still, are the Chiefs and their own native advisers. There is a Protectorate, of course, and it *is* administered by the Colonial Government. But it's only on broad lines and general principles after all."

Sir Wedgwood was a little puzzled: he could not quite see the point which his host was trying to make. He felt rather at a disadvantage in his present attire in counsel with his young friend and adviser. He played for time before thinking out a reply.

"If you will excuse me," said he, rising from his chair and pulling his dressing-gown about him, "I hear the sounds of my servants' voices. I should like to dress properly and continue this conversation later at a more opportune moment."

The District Commissioner did not rise from his seat. He continued to smoke his cigarette and to look out before him with a somewhat preoccupied air. The Professor was irritated. Who had ever heard of this young man before? He wasn't more than four or five years older than the undergraduates to whom he lectured at Cambridge, to whom he had become a sort of myth and tradition. Yet, on reflection, and before saying anything which might lead to unpleasantness, he decided to keep his own counsel. In the University from which he came he was a dominant figure, one in authority and a man whose name was familiar to savants and scholars the world over. But that cut little ice out here in Africa. The District Commissioner was the man who counted. It was he who had been set by the Government in authority over the land and the people, and his views must be listened to with respect. Of course there was the Governor, over the whole of the Colony, who had, at the instance of the Colonial Office, promised to afford him all the help that was in his power. But he had divined, even during the short time that he had stayed as his guest at Government House in the capital, that his mission was not looked upon as of supreme importance and that his subject, dilated upon at the length at which he invariably chose to deal with it, was inclined to be boring to men of action immersed in political affairs.

At length Woodward rose.

"Of course, sir, I don't want to get in your way. I only wanted to tell you that if you want to make the most of your visit to this District it will be as well for you to get on good terms with the most powerful chief in it. And he is Brima Kafari, and he wants to come and see you as soon as you are ready to receive him."

Brima Kafari! The father of Pompoli of Corpus! The Professor felt a cold shiver down his spine. But only for a moment. It was absurd to read anything sinister into the African Chief's wish to be introduced to the man who had come to study his country and his people.

The District Commissioner moved towards the gate in the veranda.

"I'm sorry to have troubled you so early." The house-boy was beginning ostentatiously to sweep the dust from one end of the veranda to the other. "I think you'll find your boys—and the orderly—quite all right when you have got to know them a little better."

He was standing on the low step outside the gate, and was turning as if to go back to his own house. He spoke slowly as if trying to formulate something further in his mind for which he had not yet quite found the words. The Professor waited. His own fears began to return.

"Yes, yes, Woodward—I'm sure I shall. I want to get dressed now and get all my things sorted out. I haven't any time to waste."

The District Commissioner turned again. The interval caused by Sir Wedgwood's speech had given him time to think the matter out.

"I'll ask the Chief to be in the 'barri' (native court house) at half-past nine. I think I'd better be there when you see him. From something his messenger said to me this morning, when he came up to arrange the interview, I think that the Chief won't be very agreeable to help you—until—until—some questions that he wants to ask are answered."

Bidding the Professor good morning the District Commissioner turned on his heel and marched briskly away in the direction of his own bungalow.

CHAPTER XI

AN UNEXPECTED TURN

To an anthropologist as keen on his subject as Sir Wedgwood Camberley the scene an hour or so later in the court of the District Commissioner at Mandu should have been of absorbing interest. Never had the learned Professor seen such a full gathering of the subjects of his studies, all under one roof. The court was an open-sided mud and thatched affair, shaped something like an ordinary English haystack. It wasn't more than thirty feet long by twenty broad, but what space on the mud floor was not occupied by the rough wooden baize-covered table of the Commissioner, his chair and that of his distinguished visitor, was packed with Africans in every variety of dress and undress wedged as closely together as sardines.

A large proportion of the assembly squatted on the floor or perched on the low mud walls which formed the sides of the "barri." Those of more exalted rank sat upon decrepit canvas deck-chairs which had seen better days, or lolled in curious-looking native-made contraptions shaped like wishbones with a short piece of wood forming the base of a triangle and another stuck out at an angle to the rear to support the contrivance.

As the Commissioner entered, followed by his guest, through a dense mass of sightseeing natives, through whom a couple of police orderlies cut a lane with their swagger sticks, the whole gathering, at the instant summons of the loud-voiced constables, rose to its feet and remained standing until they had taken their own seats at the table.

In the middle of the front row sat a stout, forbidding-looking man with a short black beard, his head covered by an elaborately embroidered cap of brilliantly dyed native-woven material which hung down in a triangular flap over his forehead. In his ears were massive gold ear-rings, and his corpulent body was swathed in the folds of a heavy red velvet gown ornamented with tarnished gold lace and paste buckles. Round his neck hung a silver chain from which was suspended a little amulet case of the same metal. In his right hand he held the brass-topped bamboo cane with the royal arms which announced to the world that he was recognised as a Paramount Chief by the Government.

Professor Camberley realised at once that this must be Brima Karifu, the father of the undergraduate, Pompoli, who had been found murdered in his rooms at Corpus. He felt distinctly uncomfortable as he looked upon the man's sinister, ugly face. He felt that the dark eyes looked out from a cruel mind, steeped in all kinds of vice, obscenity and barbarity. He recalled again with a shudder that there was a rumour that this man suspected that he might have a hand in the murder of his son. It was all very well for him to try to dismiss the idea as absurd and unthinkable. But he, as an anthropologist, knew something of the workings of the native mind. Logic for the African was not necessarily the same as for the more enlightened European, accustomed to sift evidence carefully before coming to a decision. Rumour—he had heard it often enough during his conversations with those who knew the country during the past few days—passed often enough for proven fact. Rumour had said that he, Sir Wedgwood Camberley, was suspected to know something about the death of the Corpus student. Pompoli's father was before him now, prepared, as Woodward had said, to ask him some questions concerning the death of his son. Supposing the replies he gave were unconvincing: supposing the Chief were not prepared to believe him when he asserted his ignorance of anything to do with the tragic incident.

His mind went back to the uneasy night he had spent, listening to the eerie sound of the tom-toms away in the village on the plains below. Had they not a sinister significance for him? It was all very well for the Commissioner to try to allay his fears by telling him that it was an ordinary native custom to beat the drums and spend a noisy night when one Chief came to visit in the country of another. How was he to know that that was so? Why should this Chief—the father of the murdered man—one of the two murdered men—come down all the way from his own town just to see him, to hear a few words from a white man who had met his own son far away in the white man's country, unless there were something deeper and of more baleful import in his actions?

Sir Wedgwood tried to put the uneasy thoughts from his mind as the formal greetings took place between the Chief and the District Commissioner.

"Tell the Chief how-do—plenty how-do."

The court interpreter, in flowing blue gown and orthodox red Mohammedan fez, poured out a spate of words in an unknown tongue. The Chief and his followers focused their eyes upon their Commissioner.

"And tell the Chief—too—that the big man from England—Professor Camberley—the man who knows too much about all man—tells him plenty plenty how-do as well."

The eyes of the concourse swivelled over as those of one man, and Sir Wedgwood had an uncanny feeling that the secrets of his inner heart were being read as clearly as if they had been printed on the page of a book. But what was more disturbing was that he seemed to sense that the construction which was being put upon them was distinctly unfavourable to himself. More than ever he felt that he was being put upon his trial, arraigned for his complicity in the slaying of the son of the Chief who had come into Mandu to visit the District Commissioner. He began to realise that, even if he were able to convince these people that it was absurd to imagine that he had had any hand in the deed which had led to the death of Pompoli, he would be considered, in native logic, responsible for the fate that had overtaken the African in the white man's town in which he was supposed to have so much power and authority. He remembered that the Governor had told him after dinner some stories of Africans and their customs: in particular how it was usual in some parts of the country to hold the headman of a village equally guilty with the actual murderer of a stranger within its gates and, in the days before the Government had introduced European ideas of justice, to punish him with scarcely less severity. Something about blinding or maiming was what His Excellency had suggested.

Sir Wedgwood's face paled perceptibly as he tried to smile back a greeting in exchange for the toothful grins with which Chief Brima Kafari and his followers sought to bid him welcome.

Then, as the complimentary exchange of speeches went on between the District Commissioner and the Chief and his elders, he began to regain his equanimity. It was absurd to harbour such ridiculous thoughts. He was proving that a civilised being—a highly civilised being—could conjure up more absurd fancies in his brain than the untutored savage. He should be ashamed of himself. A wakeful night in unaccustomed surroundings had played havoc with his nerves. His first sight of a big gathering of Africans, with their unfamiliar cast of countenance, had thrown him temporarily off his balance. He must pull himself together.

The District Commissioner began to speak: no further reference was made to the distinguished visitor. The Government was anxious to know how the palm kernel crop was maturing: whether there would be rice enough to go round in the "hungry season," or whether the Chief would like the Government to order some supplies from India in case of a threatened shortage.

In his replies to the questions put to him on such matters and others, Brima Kafari, through the interpreter, seemed to forget all about the Professor's presence, and Sir Wedgwood found himself reverting to his own subject and taking the unique opportunity he had of studying the cranial and other developments of the individuals who formed the mass of black humanity which crowded the little "barri" and pressed against its walls from without. He scarcely heard the conventional questions which his youthful host was plying, the long-drawn replies which the Chief gave when their purport had been conveyed by him to the interpreter, nor the translation back into English which followed.

And then, suddenly, an odd feeling of familiarity suddenly obtruded itself upon his mind. For some reason or another he saw in his mind with startling vividness a clear picture of part of the Trumpington Street as it went into Cambridge—the part that lay in the shadow of the trees in the grounds of the Leys School on the one side and those along Brookside on the other. There was nothing necessarily strange in that. He had lived in Cambridge for the greater part of his life. He must have walked that way thousands of times. But as he saw the scene this morning, in the "barri" at Mandu, he noted that the season was winter—that the time was night—that the tall trees were stripped bare of their leaves—and a street lamp shone out wanly beneath their scanty shade. He could see one or two human figures hurrying in the direction of King's Parade. Two of them—one behind the other—disappeared into the distance beyond. But there was a third—shorter than the other two—still in sight, about opposite the opening on the right into Bateman Street—who seemed to walk more slowly—almost as if waiting for something to happen.

The ceremonial conversation between the Commissioner and the Chief continued: they seemed to have lost interest in him. The Professor was left alone with his thoughts. He was puzzled, worried—almost frightened. The mind played strange tricks at times, but he could not understand what connection there could be with the scene in the "barri" this morning in Africa and Brookside on a winter's night at Cambridge. He thought again. He had been coming along Brookside himself on the night that Ogu Kalawa was murdered—on the same night on which Pompoli too had met his death in Corpus at the hands of an unknown assassin. Knowing that he was to meet Chief Brima Kafari this morning, the memory of that night had never been far from his thoughts. But the extraordinary way in which the events of that tragic time had been so suddenly recalled to him when he thought that his mind was for the time being lulled to insensibility affected him strangely. Something must have occurred to bring the scene once more before his brain.

Once more he scanned the sea of faces before him in an attempt to trace the source of the strange vision. The events of the night were outlined more clearly than ever in his mind's eye. He had been tired that day, but he had determined not to forgo the pleasure of an evening with Professor Horsell at his house in Trumpington Road. He had meant not to stay more than a couple of hours, and had noticed with dismay, just as a stimulating new discussion was beginning, that it was after half-past eleven, and he had to face another exacting round of lectures on the morrow. He also remembered the shock which he had unwittingly given his daughter when she had caught him cleaning out the revolver for which he held no licence, when matters had been complicated by the revelation in the papers that the murders had been done with a weapon of a similar type. But he had gone over all these scenes in his own mind a hundred times before, and he was still unable to trace any connection between the sudden new vision and the events of the present morning.

The exchange of courtesies was still going on between the visiting chief and the District Commissioner. The African dignitary had reached the stage at which native custom demanded the production of presents for his host and at the word of command from the "speaker" or Prime Minister of Brima Kafari—a white-bearded native dressed in a manner only slightly less sumptuous than that of his master—a small boy in a dirty white cotton shirt pushed his way through the throng at the back of the court, bearing in each hand an offering of unfortunate, skinny fowls tied together by the legs and held with their heads downwards. When these gifts had duly been laid at the feet of the Professor's host a further couple of rather moth-eaten henchmen appeared, one hauling an unwilling sheep by a rope tied none too loosely round its neck, and the other carrying a basket containing about a hundred eggs extorted from subjects in the Chief's own village to support his own exalted state in the presence of his European overlord.

Again Sir Wedgwood Camberley let his eyes run over the faces of the throng before him. None of them now showed the slightest interest in him: he was a figure of secondary importance in the day's proceedings, and he was able to scan each one at his leisure. As an anthropologist he was interested, though, in museums at home, he had already long since familiarised himself with the characteristics of most of the skulls which he saw before him on living bodies. But there was something more than mere scientific curiosity which prompted his examination. So vividly had he conjured up in his mind the picture of Brookside on the night of the Cambridge murders, that he felt certain that the vision had been prompted by something upon which his glance had fallen during the past few minutes. But, up to the time, he had been unable to trace any connection. Occasionally one of the throng before him, his interest straying momentarily from the principal actors in the scene enacted in the "barri," would fix his eyes upon those of the Cambridge professor and remain staring at him with a vacant, uncomprehending inquisitiveness. There were old men, young men, boys, girls, a few full-grown women adorned with gold and silver bracelets and necklaces of barbaric pattern—doubtless the wives of the Chief and his elders—and one or two very old women indeed. Generally, when a man, woman or child realised that they were themselves in their own turn being inspected by the distinguished visitor, they would turn shyly away and transfer their gaze ostentatiously to the main scene which was being played between the Chief and the District Commissioner. But there were exceptions, and there was one in particular.

As Sir Wedgwood Camberley ran his eye over the faces of the assembly he became aware that, for the third time that morning, there was at least one individual in the crowd who was not unduly embarrassed by his interest, and boldly returned the attention which the European was paying to him.

Scarcely realising what it was that prompted his action, the Professor determined to scrutinise this person with a little more thoroughness.

It was a young man, in the third row behind the Chief's retainers. Realising, at last, that he was attracting the Professor's notice, he himself turned away at last and concentrated his gaze once more upon the District Commissioner and his interpreter, who was still translating, to and from English and the native dialect, the formal compliments and enquiries which were still passing between Brima Kafari and young Woodward. Sir Wedgwood was suddenly struck by the fact that the man's face seemed familiar. Now that he had a chance of examining it in profile the impression became stronger still—to amount almost to a certainty. The faces of most of the negroes before him, pleasant enough for the most part, were marred by the broad, ugly noses of the race, their teeth stained and discoloured to a degree unusual in Europe by the practice of chewing tobacco and kola nuts.

None of these defects were apparent in the bold young man who had till now so boldly returned the Professor's gaze. His nose was thin and aquiline: his teeth were white and gleamed as he smiled at some pleasantry uttered by the District Commissioner or his visitor. Although he was dressed in native clothes, there was nothing gaudy or barbaric about his appearance, and Sir Wedgwood was impressed by the fact that when the District Commissioner made some joke or humorous remark, he smiled or laughed before the sally was interpreted. It was clear that he had a fluent knowledge of English. His bearing and appearance taken all round were so different from that of his neighbours that the Professor formed the opinion that he must be a native of some other tribe or race than that which formed the majority of the gathering in the "barri."

His knowledge of anthropology told him, after he had paid further attention to the shape of the man's skull, that his surmise was probably correct. He began to feel uncomfortable. Africans might be Africans, and he was not, from what he had seen of their race in the University town, greatly drawn towards them. But manners were manners, and it seemed hardly polite to study an African, at a ceremonial gathering held partly in his own honour, as if he were an ape or a monkey behind the bars of a cage at the Zoo. He was bored with the length of the proceedings and the way in which, according, he supposed, to African custom and etiquette, the same things were being said over and over again. He lowered his gaze and covered his face with his hand as if the sunlight which was now beginning to pour into the little court was too much for his eyes. This was a pretext to give himself time for thought—to try to establish some sort of connection between the waking vision he had had and the events of the morning.

Was it possible that he had seen the young man before? Cambridge was full of African students who, in his own opinion, would have been better in their own country learning subjects which were suitable to their status as an agricultural and semi-civilised people. Many of them, as he had cause to recollect, attended his own lectures. But he knew very few of them, except such as were members of his own College, even by name, and had never taken anything but a hostile interest in their being.

But there seemed to be some sort of possible link here. Perhaps the youth who had shown such interest in him had been, at some time, a student at the University. If he had seen him there he might sub-consciously have taken a note of his features. Then, suddenly seeing his face again before him when he least expected to do so, the mental shock would cause a reversion of his mind to the University town and set him thinking of well-known scenes and incidents which had occurred there.

But why should such a shock, even if it had occurred, serve to bring his mind back to one particular scene and incident?

There was some sort of explanation of that. The Chief whom he had been asked to meet that morning was the father of one of the men who had been murdered at Cambridge in the Michaelmas term: subconsciously his mind had been running on the events of which he himself had experience in connection with the death of one of them. Perhaps this, in itself, was sufficient explanation of the train of thought which had led him back to Brookside and Trumpington Street, when physically he was seated in a stuffy little African bush court more than three thousand miles from the place to which he had been mentally carried.

Try as he would he could not formulate an explanation which would wholly satisfy him, and he determined for the time being to give up the effort. Perhaps if he gave his mind a rest a suitable theory would suggest itself to him later in the day. He removed his hand from his eyes and sat upright. And as he did so he was aware of a stir in the body of the "barri." The people in the third row behind the Chief were moving—moving to make way for someone who wished to leave the court.

The Professor's interest was aroused when he saw that the person responsible for the sudden stir was the young man on whom his own interest had been so intently focused a short while before.

With difficulty he managed to extricate himself from the surrounding mass of humanity. At length he managed to reach the low wall of the "barri." A native policeman standing outside pushed the crowd outside apart to let him get clear.

"Constable! The place too hot. Keep those people back. Leave it open to make the breeze come in!"

The District Commissioner himself, more accustomed to proceedings like this than the Professor, was beginning to weary and to feel the lack of fresh air. Two or three more native policemen appeared as if from nowhere and with much shouting and beating of their swagger canes forced back the crowd to clear a lane through which the breeze, doubly welcome now that the sun was risen high in the sky, could blow through the crowded "barri."

The young man who had climbed over the low wall made a royal progress down the road cleared by the men's attentions. As he got out into the sunlight something familiar about his walk—his gait was slightly stooping for so young a man—struck the Professor. Again his thought went back to that night on Brookside. Again he saw the scene vividly out-lined before his eyes—the man over away by the trees and the wan light of the lamp—the second following behind at a distance—abreast of where Bateman Street comes out into the main road.

It was with difficulty that Sir Wedgwood Camberley repressed a cry of relief. The strain and the tension were over. In a flash he sensed the connection between his waking dream and the link between the court house at Mandu and the streets of Cambridge.

At that moment he would have been prepared to swear that the man who had just left the "barri" was one and the same person with the individual whom he had seen that night following the two undergraduates down Brookside.

CHAPTER XII

THE "C.A.D.S."

"I'M sorry, Geoffrey isn't up yet!"

Pat Frimley felt a little jealous at Dolly Camberley's words. His admiration for the Professor's daughter had by no means lessened during the vacation, and he did not feel disposed to share her with anyone, not even his friend Geoffrey Cranston.

"I mean—he's one of the 'Cads,' you know, and we're all doing this job together."

Pat Frimley was mollified: he recognised Geoffrey's right to take part in any further researches which the newly-formed society felt inclined to make.

"I expect he will be in a few days: anyway, term doesn't start for ten days, and I don't suppose he's any too keen to get back. He went sailing on the Broads."

The girl was holding a bulky letter in a foreign envelope, and the young man could see that it bore the Old Guinea stamp.

Dolly looked prettier even than usual this morning: her manner was always lively, but there seemed an additional touch of animation. Pat Frimley was glad that he had come up early for term on the pretext of putting in a week's hard work for his final examination in the summer term. When term was up Dolly had so many admirers that it wasn't too easy to get her all by herself. And he felt that the time was fast approaching when he would feel the need of a very private interview with her.

The little room in the café in Trinity Street was warm and cosy as the pair sat over morning coffee and a cigarette by the side of an electric fire: for the April morning, though the sun was shining brightly outside, was distinctly chilly. He felt convinced, from her manner, that she had some thing of importance to tell him, and the bulky envelope from Africa in her hand lent colour to his suspicions.

"You remember when we had our last meeting last term that we decided that we must help the police to trace the black man whom the policeman, and those other two fellows, saw in Brookside that night after Kalawa's body was discovered?"

Pat Frimley nodded rather guiltily. It had been part of the compact that each of them should do their best to trace the man, and put any information they got hold of in the hands of the authorities for what they might think it was worth.

"Well, what have you been doing about it?"

The girl's tone held a challenge.

"I'm afraid," said the young man, "that I really haven't done very much."

"Better tell the truth and admit that you forgot all about it."

Pat Frimley made no further defence. He admitted the impeachment. He covered his own dereliction of duty by making a countercharge against the third member of the society.

"And I bet Geoffrey hasn't done a thing either."

"I don't see," said Dolly censoriously, "that that makes things any better for you."

"And what *have you* done?"

The tone and the implication were the reverse of gallant.

"I don't know that I've done very much myself—I don't quite see how I could without the help you two promised," she emphasised the verb, "but I've got hold of something that may be going to help us."

Any interest which was remarkable in the young man's tones was due more to his preoccupation with the speaker than with the gist of her words. He was, in truth, getting a little tired of the whole subject of the Cambridge murders. They'd been discussed and re-discussed for a term and a half already, and he had not made much effort during the vacation to carry the matter any further. He wasn't a policeman, yet, and in his heart of hearts he felt that it was better to leave an affair like this to the properly constituted authorities. Knowing, however, the attitude that the girl was taking he did not venture to voice his true sentiments.

But he wasn't going to give in without a struggle.

"Do you mean that you've really *done* som ething yourself, or that you've just happened to get hold of something from somebody else?" He indicated the letter in the girl's hand.

Dolly Camberley waved the aspersion aside.

"I *have* got hold of something—from Dad—and as I wrote to him several times about what they were saying in the papers still here about the thing and asked him whether he could manage to pick anything up in the people's own country, I think I can say that I've done a bit more than the other two ' Cads.'"

Pat Frimley's waning interest in the murders began to revive. Dolly wasn't the sort of girl to go about poking out mares' nests and her whole manner this morning showed that she really thought she had something of importance to tell him.

She laid her cigarette in the saucer of her coffee cup and pulled out from the envelope she was carrying, several sheets of closely written thin foreign paper.

"I really don't quite know what to make of it," she continued. "But Dad really does seem to have had some rather funny experiences, and they *may* have something to do with the matter *you* two promised to help me go into last term."

She paused to see what effect her shot would have upon her companion. He seemed unrepentant. He had made his confession of indolence and did not propose to beat about the bush any further.

There was no one else in the café and, spreading the sheets of paper on the table before her, she began to read out passages from the letter. Her Father recounted the tale of his arrival at Mandu, and the scene in the court "barri" at which he had been introduced by the Commissioner to Pompoli's father.

"'After the Commissioner had finished his business with Brima Kafari,'" the Professor's letter continued, "'I had a few words with the Chief myself, through the interpreter. I don't know whether I misjudge these people—when I am in my own country: but I confess that the fellow seemed only too anxious to have news from someone who lived in the same town in which his unfortunate son was murdered. All the while I was talking to him I was really thinking more about the young man I had seen leave the court. I was quite certain, by then, that it was somebody's face that had recalled to me the scene I had witnessed that winter's night near Brookside. When I saw the fellow's back view, as he got up and left the court, I was quite positive *whose* face it was that had suddenly switched my mind back all those months and all that distance away. For I was not only aware that the fellow's face was familiar to me, but when he was turning his back and walking away from me, I suddenly realised that he was about the same size and stature as the man I had seen passing the end of Bateman Street behind the other two men, and that he had the same little peculiarity of walk—a sort of dip towards the right as if there was some sort of lameness in his right foot. I think I managed to satisfy the Chief that I was in no way responsible for what had happened either to his own son or to Kalawa—that I had nothing whatever to do with the policing of the University and its discipline: that that was the business of the Proctors who, themselves, could hardly be held to blame for what had happened that night. In the first place, they had no jurisdiction over a man in his own college who was not committing an offence against the regulations of the University: and, in the second, it was hardly to be expected that they would have any reason to suspect that an African student was in danger of his life round about midnight in a public place like Brookside. All this may seem rather foolish to you, but these Africans have curious mentalities—entirely different from our own, as I have always pointed out—and I had been informed that it was possible that the Brima Kafari might fancy he had some sort of grievance against me.'"

For several paragraphs the Professor reverted to his well-known prejudice against the idea of permitting African students to mix with the white races in their old University towns.

"'I calmed the old man down as well as I was able, and he ended by presenting me with fifty eggs—forty-two of which my cook assured me were not fit for human consumption—six fowls which together would have made a medium-sized table hen in an English poulterer's shop—and two pineapples. The last two gifts I rather suspected. I have heard stories about negroes tempting their enemies to their death by presenting them with pineapples in which powdered glass is concealed. I may say that a close inspection of the fruit by my cook revealed the fact that my suspicions in this direction were groundless.'

"And then," said the girl, interrupting her reading for a moment, "Dad goes on to say a lot about the nice little ways the negroes have of getting away with people they don't like. Let's see—where was I?"

She ran her finger down the page and on to the next and began to read again.

"'But I really was interested about the man I had seen. At first I said nothing about it to my host: I did not wish to make myself appear ridiculous. He might, I thought, imagine that I had got the matter of the Cambridge murders on the brain. Well, the Chief went away at last and promised to come back to see me the next day. That will be to-morrow, when this letter will have been posted, and the next mail doesn't go for ten days. That night, when I was dining with the Commissioner, I ventured to come back to the subject. I asked him whether it would be possible to trace any particular individual who had been in court amongst the crowd that morning. He seemed rather surprised at my question, and replied that he did not think there would be very much difficulty, provided I could give enough details. I then told him of my sudden vision of the scene on Brookside, and of my noting the young man in the court who had recalled the incident to my memory. At first I think he thought that I was talking nonsense. But he politely said that he would do what he could to find out if there was anything in my suspicions. He sent for the interpreter. After a little questioning the interpreter was able to place the man I had noticed. He was some sort of relative of a neighbouring Chief who had once had a palaver with Brima Kafari and also, I gathered, with the father of the other young man who was murdered, Ogu Kalawa. My host then began to realise that I was not completely unhinged and imagining things. The interpreter knew where the man could usually be found—he usually stayed with friends in the village. *He knew that he was in England last year*, sent by his father to learn office work with a shipping firm in Liverpool. A constable was sent to make discreet enquiries. All that he was able to find out was that the young fellow had left his friends that morning, packing his box *and not, contrary to his custom, telling them where he was going!'"*

CHAPTER XIII

IN UNCHARTED WATERS

THE morning was sunny and bright. But the Chief Constable of Cambridge, as he walked to his office, was not in harmony with the weather. He felt that a dark grey winter sky would better have suited his present mood. He was as concerned as anyone that no further progress had been made by the Force towards the elucidation of the mysteries of the October term and realised that unless and until something was done in the matter, a definite slur rested just as much upon the police under whose protection both town and University were placed as upon the town and University themselves. But as no progress seemed possible he could have wished that the public's memory of the matter could have been allowed to fade. Until the summer term had fairly opened he had reason to believe that no more would be said upon the point.

But his equanimity had been rudely shattered on the day on which, a fortnight back, he had received a visit from Miss Camberley, the Professor's daughter, and the undergraduate, Geoffrey Cranston, whom he had once before interviewed in connection with his general search of the Colleges in quest of clues. He had been inclined to think that the story which they had told him of the mysterious black man to whom the Professor had referred in his letter was of no importance. But the pair had declined to quit his office until he had promised to take some steps to trace the man. The information given by Sir Wedgwood was meagre in the extreme: he did not even give the name of the mysterious stranger, though, as the District Commissioner's interpreter seemed aware of his identity, that should not have been impossible. He had written to Scotland Yard, and was surprised and a little annoyed that sufficient weight had been attached to the clue, if it could be called one, for a cable to be sent to the Old Guinea Police asking if they would go further into the matter.

The police in West Africa had at once acted: the man of whom the Professor spoke had been identified, and his name had been cabled home. Scotland Yard had furnished him with this. It was Abu Bokari which did not convey very much to the Chief Constable. He had had a letter the day before from Scotland Yard informing him that all shipping offices in Liverpool had been circularised asking for information as to a native of Old Guinea who might, during the previous twelve months, have entered their service as a junior clerk or apprentice. The firms, the letter went on, had been asked to communicate any facts which might transpire direct to the Cambridge police.

So there would be more useless stuff to deal with in the office this morning. He sighed as he reached the station and went up the steps. When he saw the baskets on his desk his worst fears were realised. There were piles of opened letters in them, about five times as many as usual. There was little doubt that they were the replies from the Liverpool firms. A glance at the top ones, as he wearily seated himself at his desk, confirmed his worst fears. A cursory run over the contents of the baskets convinced him that there were more shipping offices in the city than in the rest of the towns in the country put together, and that at least half the population of Old Guinea was in one way or another employed in them. But in the lists of names there was not one which could be stretched, by any exercise of the imagination, into a semblance of that of the missing Abu Bokari.

The Chief Constable had only just finished wading through the papers when the police orderly knocked on his door and announced Geoffrey Cranston. It was with some difficulty that he managed to summon up sufficient politeness to give him even a perfunctorily civil greeting.

"Good morning, sir," said the young man as he imperturbably produced a cigarette and seated himself in the visitor's chair without asking his host's permission or even offering him a cigarette. "Have you heard anything yet from Liverpool?"

"Have I heard anything from Liverpool?" He indicated with a sweep of his arm the letters which overflowed from the brimming baskets before him.

"By Jove—that's luck!" cried Cranston. "This *is* a bit of luck!"

The Chief Constable could have called it many things, equally terse, but nothing like as polite.

"Oh—what makes you think that?"

"Why—we ought to be able to get something out of all this."

The Chief Constable restrained his wrath. After all, this zeal in the interests of public justice and the honour of the University town was really highly to be commended. But Deepcut was in no commendatory mood.

"Before you are so sure of that, young man, I'd like you to have a look at a few of these."

He indicated the letters on the desk. Geoffrey Cranston seized a handful with an eagerness which the Chief Constable found it hard to understand.

"Can you make anything of those—any of them—anything that's of the slightest use to us?"

His tone was a mixture of sarcasm and despair. But his young visitor was undismayed.

"Why, what do you mean, sir? Aren't there enough names here to make a start on?"

"Enough—indeed: but how do you propose to make a start? You've only got a few of them there: there seem to be hundreds of them. But I'll bet my boots you don't find a single name like Abu Bokari amongst them; and nor there is—amongst the whole lot."

To Deepcut's astonishment the young man laughed.

"Abu Bokari? The name the West African people cabled home? But did you think you would? If, as we suspect, this fellow came home thinking of doing in his two pals from the same country, is it likely that he'd use his own name? Besides, though

I'm not a policeman—yet—I daresay I know a bit more about West Africa than you do. Not that I've been there myself yet: but I've read stacks of books about the place, and I almost feel I had."

Geoffrey Cranston's tone was condescending—that of the expert talking to the amateur, and the Chief Constable would have liked to kick him. He'd not had an University education himself, and he was glad of it: it could turn young men, otherwise quite decent, into infernally insufferable young puppies. But he got the better of his own feelings; and it was possible that there was a grain of truth in what Geoffrey Cranston had said. Besides, when all was said and done, he really ought to feel a certain amount of gratitude to the young man and his friends who had still sufficient enthusiasm left in the matter to be willing to try to assist the police in the difficult task which confronted them.

But he could not give in without some pretence of a fight.

"What's knowledge of West Africa got to do with it, any way?"

The young man became more serious.

"What I mean is—these fellows from Old Guinea—natives, of course, and as black as your hat and all that often give themselves white men's names, especially when they come 'home'—as they call it—meaning England." He laughed. "For instance, I believe I'm right in saying that there are more Johnsons and Jones's and Campbells in Freetown in Sierra Leone than you'll find in the London Telephone Directory."

The Chief Constable lay back in his chair amazed.

"Well—suppose that is so—which I must say never knew before—how's that going to help us here?"

Geoffrey Cranston took up one of the letters and referred to the schedule which accompanied it.

"See here," said he, "in this letter from the West African Fruit Line: look at the list of native employees—in the office—at the docks—even on the ships themselves. 'Smith, Jones, Robinson,' all English enough, in sound. But do you suppose that those are the names they were born with?"

A light began to dawn on the Chief.

"You mean that this man, if he ever was here at all, had an alias?"

The undergraduate nodded.

"Of course," said he. "They seem to think that giving themselves white men's names makes them a bit more like white men than nature has made them. Besides—if this fellow—as we are supposing he did—came over here to do the dirty on a couple of his pals—is it likely he'd parade his own name while he was here? I should have thought even the simplest criminal would have thought of having a sort of pen-name in the circumstances."

Deepcut began to warm up: the young man's enthusiasm was infectious. After all, the crimes were still unsolved, he ought to welcome the efforts of anyone at all to help him since he could think of no further means of helping himself.

"So you mean that, if we disregard the evidence of names as vital, we may be able to winnow these lists down by other means—the length of time the men were in the country—when they left—and so on?"

The young man agreed.

"That's just what I meant: especially the date they left the country—if they ever did. I see the firms have given those dates—where there are any."

"The questionnaire from Scotland Yard was pretty comprehensive."

The Chief Constable basked in the glory reflected on him from headquarters.

With a sigh he determined to devote the morning, with the help of his new friend, to the analysing of the lists from Liverpool.

It was a long task and a dreary one, and at times the Chief Constable would have liked to give up: the enthusiasm which Geoffrey Cranston had momentarily bred in him was waning, and he began to have serious doubts as to whether the game was worth the candle. But he was ashamed to betray his feelings, for the undergraduate showed no signs of tiring.

"It's very good of you to come and help me like this." He looked at the clock. "But surely I must be keeping you from your work—lectures or something?"

Geoffrey Cranston laughed.

"I don't think missing a day will do me much harm. And this is real work, isn't it?"

From the bottom of his heart the Chief Constable agreed with his visitor, but he did not say so too emphatically.

At the end of a couple of hours of diligent searching and comparison there remained two names which might, from the attendant circumstances, have covered the identity, if it was hidden, of the missing Abu Bokari. A young man from Old Guinea, rejoicing in the name of Absalom Perkins had been taken on as an apprentice by the Green Funnel Line in September the year before and had left, without explanation, four months later, at a time which would coincide with the appearance of the mysterious negro stranger in Cambridge. The other suspect was a youth named Ephraim Smith, employed as a premium pupil for practically the same period by the iron ore firm of Parker & Browne, which maintained its own line of steamers plying to and from the Coast. In his case the firm, on the absconding of Smith, had written to his parents or guardians in Old Guinea informing them that the premium was confiscated. No reply had been received and the secretary was in doubt as to whether the company's letter had ever been delivered.

"So you see we *have* made some progress after all."

It was nearly one o'clock, and the Chief Constable's stomach was as unerring as a watch.

"I think," said he, "that that is enough for one morning. I'm very grateful to you for your help. With the information we have got out the Yard may be able to make further enquiries and test whether there's anything in the theory."

There was a knock at the door. The police orderly entered hastily.

"A Mr. Frimley—with your permission, sir—to see Mr. Cranston: he says it's urgent."

The constable's words were hardly out of his mouth when Pat Frimley, excited and perspiring, burst into the room.

"I hope you'll excuse me, sir—but I've got something important to tell Mr. Cranston: and it may concern you too."

Before the Chief Constable had time to recover from the effects of this unexpected intrusion Frimley went on:

"It's a cable—Dolly—Miss Camberley's—had. It's about her father. He's been shot in the back—by some native. He's not dead—but—but—it's very, very serious, and I want you to help."

CHAPTER XIV

"EX AFRICA..."

THE Chief Constable was disgusted: that was a mild way of expressing the state of his feelings when, his time for lunch already being five minutes past owing to the ridiculous enthusiasm of an undergraduate whose activities he felt could have been more usefully employed in preparing for examinations than in playing the part of an amateur detective, the longed-for meal was still further postponed by the post-haste arrival of Frimley with the news of the disaster to Professor Camberley.

Not that Deepcut had any personal feelings either for or against Sir Wedgwood. His only professional contact with him had been when he had sent a subordinate to make enquiries when the distinguished anthropologist was suspected of being in possession of a firearm for which he had omitted to take out a licence. And even that little episode had ended triumphantly for the Professor.

But he did his best to disguise his feelings in deference to the real concern which was displayed upon the new arrival's features.

"I'm very sorry to hear that—very sorry."

He did not think it worth while to add that he might have felt a great deal more sorrow had the announcement of the sad news come at a less inopportune moment.

Geoffrey Cranston was startled.

"My God—we are getting into a mess!"

"And how," ventured the Chief Constable, resenting his

apparent inclusion in the plural of the personal pronoun, "do you make that out? My district doesn't include the whole of West Africa. Cambridge town *and* University," he added meaningly, "are quite enough to go on with. I'm sorry to hear what you have told us—very sorry—I know how much respected the Professor is in both, but I really can't see what it has to do with me."

Pat Frimley was apologetic.

"I didn't mean that at all, sir. It was only because I knew that Mr. Cranston was with you that I came here—to tell him as soon as I could. And I did think, too," he added as an afterthought, "that you might be interested as well; for there's a chance that it might be mixed up with these Cambridge affairs. You see, sir, it was an open secret that Professor Camberley had no special use for natives. He was in their own country when this happened and, what is more, from what we have heard, has lately been visited by a Chief whose son was one of the men who was murdered here in the October term. But what makes it still more remarkable," he said, turning to Cranston, "is that Sir Wedgwood was shot—in the back—and by a revolver."

The Chief Constable laughed: these amateurs were very good at making lightning calculations and deductions and arriving at startling conclusions.

"If you two gentlemen are going out to Africa to be policemen—some of your duties at least will have to do with the police—I think I should advise you to be a little more careful what facts you act on. If you're going to deduce that all crimes, which are at all similar in any respect, are somehow connected with each other, you'll land yourself in some funny places."

He laughed again and was pleased to see that he had somewhat unsettled the two young men's composure. It was now getting on for a quarter past the hour, and the pangs of hunger were not growing any the less apparent. It was only poetic justice that these unwelcome intruders upon the short space of leisure which he could call really his own in the midst of his official day should, in their turn, suffer some annoyance.

"We'll go, sir," said Frimley at last, a little nettled and in tones which did not disguise his feelings. "Only, I should have thought that you yourself would have been as interested as my friend to hear the news. It's quite true that this may be a coincidence: but on the other hand it mayn't: and there's precious little that the police have had to go upon in these Cambridge murders. Africa is a mysterious sort of country—we all know that—and odd things happen there. I've often read things in books that you'd scarcely believe to be true."

The Chief Constable was not going to have his lunch still further delayed by listening to a lot of cock-and-bull stuff about Africa. It wasn't his province and, anyway, he'd read enough novels—Edgar Wallace's in particular—to know how easy it was for anyone who wrote books to make mountains out of molehills and get mystery upon mystery out of things that weren't really mysterious at all.

"I dare say you have, my lad. But when you've been a policeman as long as I have—which please God you won't—you'll learn that it isn't often that any of the things we come up against can be called really mysterious. Just plain common sense—and hard work—and plenty of it."

"I'm very much obliged to you, sir, for what you've done this morning."

Geoffrey Cranston's manner was distinctly frigid. The Chief Constable's interest in the case seemed to be waning. Surely a man in his position should be above watching the clock and being a stickler for regular office hours when volunteers were ready to come forward and give him information which might assist him in his weary task of tracking down the perpetrators of mysterious crimes.

The Chief Constable was relieved to find that the two young men really were making a move. He registered a silent determination not to be caught again like this by amateur investigators. He would see that in future they worked off their enthusiasm on his subordinate, Inspector Worplesdon. Or he would send them off for a personal interview with Scotland Yard. They wouldn't be quite so softly treated there.

"There's no need to thank me: I'm here to do what I can. Though, frankly, I don't think we've got very much further this morning. And—between you and me——" His manner became grave and portentous, and he dropped his glance lest his hearers should sense in his eyes the facetiousness which underlay his words. "All right, Worplesdon: come in—I've nearly done." His subordinate entered, softly closed the door and waited. "I've got a new theory—altogether new. I don't believe these Cambridge crimes *were* committed by a nigger at all. I believe the chap who bumped off these two young men was a *white man*!"

Pat Frimley and Geoffrey Cranston looked at each other in amazement. Was the Chief Constable just bluffing—making them ridiculous in revenge for the trouble they had caused him that morning? Or did he really know more than he would admit? Were the Cambridge police and the authorities at Scotland Yard all the time working quietly at some definite clue, saying nothing about it until the time came for them to pounce the more surely upon the man around whom they were weaving their net of unescapable evidence? They knew that such things had happened before. But if that hypothesis were the correct one, why should Deepcut, in an unguarded moment, let the cat out of the bag after so many months of secret, unsuspected tracking? It might, of course, mean that things were so far advanced that the police were actually about to come out into the open and arrest their man, and that there was no need for any further concealment.

But it was two decidedly puzzled young men who descended the steps of the Cambridge Police Station that morning, and hastily made their way to the house in Park Crescent to condole with Dolly Camberley, and await further and more reassuring news of the Professor of Experimental Anthropology.

CHAPTER XV

ON PARKER'S PIECE

"IT'LL be all right, Dolly. Your father's as strong as a horse. If it had been a really bad wound he'd have died at once."

As Pat Frimley reflected on the words after he had spoken them he realised that the argument for the Professor's safety was not very convincing. Even if the wound had not been in such a position as to inflict death at once, it did not necessarily mean that complications might not ensue later which would entail a fatal result. His heart ached for the girl as she sat, her head in her hands to hide her eyes, swollen with tears, on the sofa in the stately Victorian drawing-room in Park Terrace on which, in his hours of leisure, Sir Wedgwood Camberley had been in the decidedly un-Victorian habit of stretching his long limbs.

"Besides," put in Geoffrey Cranston, feeling that he must add his own contribution towards comforting the distraught girl, "if it really were—so *very* serious—we'd have heard more by now."

This remark was even less convincing than his friend's attempt at consolation, and Dolly Camberley, still weeping silently behind the cover of her hands, made no attempt to reply. The two young men grew more and more uncomfortable. This was their first encounter with beauty in distress—real distress—and they were by no means enjoying the experience.

"I wish—oh, how I wish—Dad had never gone to that horrible country. It would have been a terrible enough thing to happen at home. But there—out there—amongst all those people—black people that he hates so much—oh, it's terrible—terrible. And no proper doctor either."

Both the young men were anxious to relieve the girl's feelings on this point.

"That's where you're wrong," cried Pat Frimley, almost triumphantly. "We've read the latest Government report on Old Guinea. And it says that on every station in West Africa where there are white men, there's a doctor—or—*nearly* every station," he ended lamely, but wishing to be entirely truthful.

Dolly Camberley was not going to be comforted in this fashion. The only thing that would reassure her would be a further cable with news of her father's recovery, or steps in that direction. And much as she longed for the second wire, she dreaded to hear the rat-tat of the telegraph boy on the door, for she realised and feared that the message might contain something which she might dread to read.

"If only—if only—we could hear something," she finally burst out, knowing all the time that she feared that her wish might come true and that it would not be answered in the way in which she hoped and prayed it might. "Can't one—nowadays—telephone—by wireless—anywhere in the world?"

Pat Frimley and Geoffrey Cranston looked at one another rather sheepishly. They had not been to West Africa, and they sometimes, fervently wished that they never might have to go there. But they had learned enough from handbooks and reports of the Colony to which they would perhaps be posted that such communications were as impossible in the twentieth century as they were in the days when the settlement was founded. Even had it been possible to get through a direct message to the capital on the Coast, they were quite positive that there were no such facilities for getting in touch with the bush up-country. The most that could be done, even in Edwardsville, was to send a wire or a telephone message up the line to the nearest station to the place which one wished to reach, and to have the communication sent on by a native runner to its exact destination, which might take a day or even more to reach. Even the date on the cablegram which had already been received did not convey very much, as the exact time of the unfortunate occurrence was not stated.

The information which the youths were able to give the Professor's daughter was not encouraging, and they wished she had never asked the question so insistently as to demand an answer.

After a few more desultory and unsuccessful attempts at conversation and leading the girl's thoughts into some other channel, Geoffrey Cranston despaired of being able to be of any further assistance.

"I'm very sorry, Dolly: you know that. And I'm awfully sorry, too, that I can't do very much. I should try to rest if I were you. I really must get off now to my digs. I've got an awful lot of stuff to get up for to-morrow."

The information surprised Pat Frimley. Cranston was not in the habit of letting his work interfere with his afternoons on the river. But he saw that there was nothing much that his friend could do in the circumstances, and he was glad to be left alone, even at such an unpropitious time, with the girl he loved.

The afternoon wore on, and there were still no signs of any further message. At last, tired out with grief and anxiety, Dolly Camberley fell into a fitful sleep on the couch, and Frimley, alarmed at the ravages which the sad news had already wrought on her pretty face, usually so gay and so animated, kissed her gently on the lips.

* * *

"Good-night, sir."

It was a sultry summer evening, and the Chief Constable, unable to sleep, thought that a turn in the fresh air might do him good. He acknowledged the salute of the constable he met in St. Andrew's Street as he made for Parker's Piece.

It was past midnight, and there was not a soul about. As he came out into the open, after passing down the little lane alongside the University Arms which leads into Park Terrace, he filled his lungs with the air which blew up across the Piece, rustling the leaves of the trees and heralding a coming storm. This was some way off yet, though even now flashes of intermittent lightning could be seen over the mass of houses between him and the railway station. But as yet there was not a sound of the thunder which would come, and he was grateful for the stir in the air which preceded it. The Piece, at this time of night, was as empty as the streets of the town, and he lay down presently, and luxuriously stretched his limbs at full length on the cool turf spread like a soft cushion beneath him. Gratefully he drew in the night air: despite the coming storm it was fresh and cool compared with the atmosphere of the stuffy streets throughout the day, and of the dust-laden police office with its files of papers in which Fate compelled him to pass so much of his time.

Thoughts of the office led his mind back once more to the mysterious murders of the two undergraduates which were still as far from explanation as ever. Not all the help offered by the much vaunted sleuths of Scotland Yard had been able to shed any light whatever on the mysterious crimes, and he began to fear that they might be eventually added to the ever-growing list of unpunished murders. But there was a difference. Chief Constable Deepcut knew quite well that in many cases of crime which the police are bound officially to label unsolved are only so in the sense that not sufficient evidence is forthcoming to enable them to lay their hands upon the criminal with the certainty that they will be able to prove their case in a court of law. As the law of the country stood, once a man had been tried by his peers and acquitted, he could never be re-arrested and tried again on the same charge whatever evidence might come later into the hands of the authorities. In many cases which the public imagined to be entirely unexplained the police had such strong suspicion as almost to amount to proof of the identity of the culprit. But there were just those missing parts in the chain of legal evidence, which would be accepted by a judge and jury, which rendered it inadvisable that the chance of an acquittal should be run. The police preferred to abstain from making a definite charge and testing the issue and thus running the risk of putting their man beyond their reach for ever, even if they were lucky enough at a later stage to be able to produce the missing links.

The Cambridge cases, as the Chief Constable reflected, were not in this category. So far as he knew the Yard had not even a suspicion as to the identity of the murderer or murderers, nor whether the two crimes were the work of the same assassin. The weapon used in each case had been similar. But that did not necessarily prove that the two victims had met their deaths at the same hands.

There had been a momentary suggestion that the Professor of Experimental Anthropology was implicated. That suggestion, based on Sir Wedgwood's undisguised dislike of the coloured section of the University, and the fact that an anonymous letter writer had hinted that he was in possession of a revolver without a licence, seemed, at this distance of time, too ridiculous ever to have been seriously entertained.

Yet the news which Frimley had brought to Cranston that morning in his office had to some extent revived the theory that there might be some connection, however slender, between Sir Wedgwood Camberley and the Cambridge murders. On further reflection the Chief Constable was unable to trace it. It seemed like a nightmare. Respectable University Professors simply didn't go about the Colleges or the streets of the town at night shooting undergraduates in the back, whether they were white or black. Strange things could happen in Africa—did often happen in the Dark Continent—to white men who went exploring in unknown regions. The attack on the Professor was probably the freak of a native who had run amok, mistaking Sir Wedgwood for some police officer sent by the Government to track him down for some misdemeanour he had committed. It might have happened to anyone. It was a mere misfortune for the Professor that he had been wrongly identified with the law, and an accident pure and simple that he should have got the wound which was intended for the real police officer. The public might not think so when they read of the event in the newspapers. The sensation-mongering journalists would see to it that no effect was lost by omitting to include a reference to the fact that the Professor was known to be operating in territory adjacent to the Chiefdom ruled over by the father of one of the young men who had met their death at Cambridge.

The air became sultrier, but so far there was no hint that the storm would break over the town very soon. The police officer began to feel drowsy. His wife was away on holiday with the children. There was no real need for him to return to his home that night. He felt that he would be unable to sleep if he did. He had often, on hiking tours with his son, slept in the open. It would do him no harm to do so again. If the storm really did break eventually with any violence he would soon wake up, and he could always make for the little pavilion near the University Arms Hotel and remain there until it had finished. Taking off his coat he folded it carefully and placed it under his head to serve as a pillow. He smiled to himself as he dozed off to sleep. It would be rather amusing if one of his own men, punctilious in the execution of his duty, were to search the Piece that night for vagrants and pounce on his potential prize, only to find that it was the Chief Constable of Cambridge who had got into his clutches.

The storm broke about an hour later. The thunder clouds gathered over the town and broke pouring cascades of water into the streets and on to the open spaces of the town. The lightning played furiously over the Colleges and the few persons whose business kept them out of doors during the early hours of the morning ran hastily to shelter from the downpour in doorways, to watch the play of the electric flashes over the sleeping houses.

But there was one man in the town who did not heed the roar of the thunder, the brilliance of the lightning, nor the torrents of rain which fell on Parker's Piece. For towards dawn, when the storm was abating, a constable on his rounds, crossing the Piece towards the middle of the town, came upon a body in the middle of the grass. It was a dead body, and there was a gaping bullet wound in the chest of the man who lay prone upon the common. And the man that the policeman found was the Chief Constable of Cambridge.

CHAPTER XVI

"THE CASE IS ALTERED"

THE news of the discovery of the dead body of Chief Constable Deepcut on Parker's Piece caused a profound sensation in Cambridge. It was not that he had many friends to mourn the sudden loss. He had been by no means unpopular, but he was a reserved and retiring man, and took part in very few of the social activities of the town after his day's work was done. He used often to say that the fewer friends a man in his position made in the sphere of his official activities the better: you never knew. Human nature was fallible. The best of men occasionally did something wrong—or something which the law of the land said was wrong, and awkward consequences might possibly ensue in cases in which official police duty cut across the ties of friendship and acquaintance.

The inquest had revealed little that was of use in tracing the murderer. Police Constable Perkins, who made the tragic discovery, stated that it was about 5 a.m. when he crossed Parker's Piece, which was on his regular beat. The medical evidence tended to show that Deepcut had been dead about four hours when his body was found, which fixed the time of the crime at about 1 a.m., at least an hour after the constable had wished him good night before he reached the Piece. There was a wound in the heart caused by a bullet from a Webley revolver of Service pattern. It was clear that the victim had been shot whilst asleep. The police had searched the Piece carefully, but no tracks had been found to help to bring home the crime to the guilty person. The firm grass of the Piece was soaked with the rain of the night before and its spongy condition did not conduce to the preservation of clear footprints. Before the police had time to throw a cordon round the part where the outrage had occurred, whilst the surgeon made his preliminary inspection, many persons had congregated, and there would have been very little chance, in any case, of tracing the way by which the criminal had come and gone.

The members of the public were not long, aided by the Press, in connecting the new crime with the murders of the two negro undergraduates of the October term, though there seemed little real evidence on which such an assumption could be fairly made. It was true that Deepcut, as Chief Constable of the town, had been in charge of the enquiry in those cases: but most of the work had actually been done by his subordinate, Inspector Worplesdon, and the men detailed by Scotland Yard.

There was not even an identity of weapons used in the several crimes. The two Africans had met their deaths as the result of shots fired in the back by a small automatic pistol. The Chief Constable had been killed by a shot through the heart from the front by a revolver of heavy calibre. Some thought that the fact that the murderer had had time to get away with his fire-arm was unfortunate: that the discovery of the weapon would have given the police a better chance in the coming search. Others thought that it was lucky that the man had taken his revolver with him. Such a thing would not be easily disposed of, and there was a chance that records existed which might enable the authorities to establish its source. But the Scotland Yard officials did not attach much importance to either point.

Enquiries on the subject of a possible motive led nowhere. Deepcut had only held the position of Chief Constable of Cambridge for three years prior to his death, and during that time had been fortunate enough to have very few cases of violent crime to deal with. Burglars, of whom he had prosecuted a few, are not particularly prone to revenge themselves after their release from prison upon the officers who had prosecuted them, though anonymous letters threatening dire retribution were a not uncommon feature of some cases. But the officers from Scotland Yard did not neglect this possible clue, and had managed to account for all burglars and violent criminals, whose apprehension was due to Deepcut's actions, who had been released from prison during two years preceding the Chief Constable's death. The rest were still safely behind prison walls.

Similar researches were made in connection with the post which Deepcut had held in Staffordshire before his promotion to the University city, but again with negative results.

Enquiries set afoot with regard to the dead man's private life were equally unsuccessful. There were very few people with whom he had had even slight disagreements, and none who would be in the least likely to seek revenge upon him by resorting to murder.

One could not rule out the possibility that the crime had been the work of a lunatic or of someone temporarily insane. The records of asylums throughout the country were carefully searched, but nothing transpired to lead the police to believe that a homicidal maniac was known to be at large either at or near Cambridge or anywhere else.

Public opinion, despite the lack of evidence, began to veer back to the theory that the murder had some mysterious connection with the deaths of the undergraduates Kalawa and Pompoli. Inspector Worplesdon, who temporarily took over the duties of his chief, began to be drawn in the same direction. But assuming that there was something in the theory he, as well as the London officers, were quite at a loss as to where to begin their investigations. There had been a complete lack of success in tracing the previous criminal or criminals. There again no motive could be definitely hazarded which would give the enquirers a point of departure. Work upon the previous cases had virtually ceased. The dossiers, of course, were still open: but there was simply no trail which it seemed possible to follow with any prospect of a successful conclusion.

Both Frimley and Cranston, who were known to have had an interview with the deceased the morning before the murder, were interviewed at length by the Scotland Yard officers and Worplesdon in the hope that, as their contact with him had been so recent, something might emerge in this direction which would serve to indicate a trail which might be followed.

* * *

"But there wasn't much we could tell them that was likely to be of much use."

The punt, containing Pat, his friend Cranston, and Dolly Camberley, was paddled slowly past the Backs on a glorious late May afternoon. The girl had had reassuring news of her father, who seemed to be well on the way to recovery. There had been no time for a letter to reach her yet: but the wording of the cables indicated that the Professor had no intention, despite his accident, of giving up the work which he had planned. He even appeared to be contemplating prolonging his stay in Africa to make up for the time which he had lost owing to the occurrence. This proof of her father's obstinacy amused Dolly, even though she was a little nervous that he should consider remaining in a country where he was quite likely, owing to his known views, to be unpopular and where someone had actually gone so far as to attempt his murder. But she could comfort herself with the assurance that his eyes were now fully open to any danger that he might be running, and with the knowledge that the Government of the Colony would take renewed steps to assure the safety and welfare of its distinguished guest.

"I shouldn't have thought there was anything at all: I don't see how there could be."

Dolly Camberley answered Pat Frimley in tones loud enough to drown temporarily the strains of the portable gramophone in a passing punt which raucously blared one of the latest "hot" dance tunes, strangely out of keeping with the noble aspect of the pinnacles of King's College Chapel.

"All the same," put in Geoffrey Cranston, who was punting, "I can't help thinking, whatever anyone may say, that there *is* some sort of connection between all these things: the murder of the two niggers, the attempt to kill Sir Wedgwood, and the death of the Chief Constable."

It was easy to make such a remark in conversation: but when the matter came to be discussed, for the hundredth time since the event of two or three days ago, it wasn't so easy to get very much further than the bare assertion.

"Anyway," continued Cranston, "the police don't seem to have given up the idea entirely. When I went round there again this morning—old Worplesdon sent for me—all hot and bothered as usual, and afraid of seeming too much of an ass before the detectives who were down again from London—I was told that the wretched niggers in residence this term have been having a lively time. They've all been interviewed and asked if they've got any arms of any kind. I believe they've gone as far as getting the gyps to search their rooms when they're out to see if they've been lying. But I gathered that nothing at all suspicious has been found."

"As *none* of the blacks up now come from Old Guinea, it seems to me rather a waste of time."

Dolly Camberley nodded approval of Pat Frimley's remark.

The three were silent for a time. It didn't seem to be possible to get very much further with the one subject about which people in Cambridge, whether of the town or of the University, seemed at present to be able to talk. The punt went on in leisurely fashion and, for a while at least, they tried to forget the disturbing incidents which were now becoming so unpleasantly common in their lives. At last a spot for mooring, under the shade of a convenient willow which warded off the fierce rays of the blazing sun, presented itself.

"I vote we tie up here." Geoffrey Cranston had had enough punting for the time being. The desire for a breather, as much as the pangs of hunger which were now asserting themselves, prompted his suggestion.

The resolution was carried unanimously, and the punt was soon securely fastened, with the pole at one end and the painter at the other, against the low bank of the pleasant stream.

Pat Frimley busied himself in setting up the temporary table.

"Don't see why Geoffrey should do all the work. I'll get busy now."

Cranston laughed scornfully. His shirt-sleeves were rolled up, and though his grey flannel trousers showed signs of damp where he had suffered as the result of the passing of a splashy and inexperienced sculler, he was hot and panting.

"Call that *work?* You can do a bit of poling on the way back and I'll sacrifice myself by the arduous job of getting the table ready for tea."

"Rather early days to talk of tea before we've even had lunch," cried Dolly Camberley as she opened the lunch basket and began to lay the table.

"Damn—I've dropped one of the knives."

The exclamation came from the girl who began to fumble at the bottom of the boat beneath the table spread across its sides.

Pat Frimley, who was sitting on the broad cushion beside her, at once came to the rescue.

"Here—let me. You'll get yourself in an awful muck fishing about in the bilge water, or whatever you call it. But perhaps the water Geoffrey shipped isn't called bilge: some other name, perhaps."

"I could suggest a good many other names," said Cranston in a minatory tone, "if a lady weren't present." He made a sweeping bow towards Dolly. "We'll just see how much water *you* manage to ship on the way back. And besides, it was that sculler fellow we passed."

"Stop wrangling, you two," cried Dolly.

She and the young man beside her were still groping in the darkness beneath the table in their endeavours to retrieve the precious knife.

"Hallo! What's this? I can't find the knife, but I seem to have got hold of something else."

Quickly she withdrew her hand and, unclosing it before the two young men, disclosed a small object.

"What in the world is that? Looks like a bullet."

Pat Frimley bent forward excitedly to examine the thing which the girl held in her palm. Cranston got up and stooped forward. Dolly's words had brought back the minds of all three to the subject they had been discussing that morning.

"By Jove," cried Cranston, "it *is* a bullet—and a new one—like the ones that fit a Webley Service revolver!"

CHAPTER XVII

THE BULLET

"I'M sorry to have to trouble you," said Acting Chief Constable Worplesdon, and his looks did not belie his words. It was bad enough to have to assume, at such short notice, the duties of an office for which he was so little prepared after the tragic death of Chief Constable Deepcut, without any further complications which might ensue in connection with the unsolved murders of the negro students. "But I don't see what else I could have done."

Chief Inspector Bramley, who had come hurriedly down from Scotland Yard on Worplesdon's summons, nodded his head sympathetically. It took a good deal to rattle him. Mysterious crime—sometimes at long length solved, sometimes not—never worried him now unduly. He had had his baptism of fire many years before, and things like this were all in the day's work for him. But he could appreciate the position of his companion.

"It was certainly odd that the thing was found by one of the young fellows who was taking such an interest in the clearing up of the Kalawa and Pompoli affairs. You're satisfied that the boatman is telling the truth? I don't mean that he would tell you lies willingly. But people—in the country especially—are very imaginative, and they sometimes read a lot more into things than the facts themselves warrant, and jump a bit too fast to conclusions."

Worplesdon shook his head.

"Brimpton's not that sort. I've known him a good many years. He'd be rather inclined, if anything, to go to the other extreme—

say he'd forgotten things sooner than possibly get himself, even indirectly, concerned with the police. He said that it was the first time that that particular punt—No. 56—had been let out this year. It's an old one—got a bit knocked about last summer term. And it needed a certain amount of repairing before he could feel justified in hiring it out again. As it *was* one of his oldest boats it had been left for repairs till the last. Those that didn't need so much attention were mostly looked after during the winter. He had, in fact, thought of scrapping No. 56. But this summer has turned out so fine that he wanted to get all his craft put into commission. These boat people don't do too well these days: undergraduates haven't got the money to spend that they had before the war; and a man in his trade has literally got to make all the money he can while the sun shines."

"He can't swear to letting it out to any particular black fellow last year?"

Chief Inspector Bramley pulled meditatively at his pipe: he was as puzzled as his provincial colleague. Worplesdon shook his head again.

"No—he can't. There are lots of them up here nowadays, more—I think—than, there were before the war. This particular boat, he knows, was not hired to any one man or party of men. It was just let out casually for the hour or the day. All he can say is that lots of black fellows used it from time to time. But he can't recollect their names—or their Colleges. Not that it would, to my way of thinking, help us much if he could. You remember I told you that young Cranston told us that at his last interview with him—the morning of the day he was shot—Deepcut said that he did not see any reason why the crimes shouldn't have been committed by a white man. It's pure guesswork, of course. It is, all of it, in these cases, worse luck."

The Acting Chief Constable sighed heavily.

"As for your saying," he continued, "that it's funny that the bullet didn't turn up before: I don't think there's anything very strange in that. There are lots of corners and laths and things in the framework of a punt where a small thing like that could get tucked away and stay hidden, even if men had been working on other parts of the boat."

Chief Inspector Bramley opened a small cardboard box which lay on the desk between them. Without touching the revolver bullet which it contained, he pulled up the cotton wool in which it lay embedded so as to turn the object right round.

"It doesn't look very rusty," said he, examining it at closer quarters. "You'd have thought that if it had been there all the winter it would have shown more discoloration."

Worplesdon sighed again: it was becoming a marked mannerism of his these days.

"You would have thought, too," he said ponderously, "that it wouldn't have been possible for one undergraduate to be murdered in the open street and another in his rooms in College nearly nine months ago and the police, even now, not have the slightest clue as to who did it or how it was done."

Bramley laughed. It was no good getting into this despairing state. It was part of a policeman's job to crack hard nuts, and he'd cracked a few in his day.

"It beats me," said he, "to think *why* it is that these fellows, or you, should necessarily think that this finding of a Webley bullet in a punt should have anything to do with the October crimes. The gun used in those affairs wasn't a Webley, anyway. It's true that a Webley was used in the case of the Chief Constable. But we haven't any sort of real right to connect up his death with the other two, have we?"

"I suppose not," said the other despondently. "But whatever anyone may say"—his tone was apologetic as he saw that his visitor might think that he himself was included in the general implication—"I've got a sort of feeling all along that Deepcut's death, and the murders of these two blacks, *and* the attack on the Professor in Africa *are* joined up, and that if we could only get a line on one of them we'd be half-way towards solving the whole thing."

The Chief Inspector remained silently puffing at his pipe for a few seconds.

"You've checked up anyone in this town who's got a licence to have an Army revolver?"

"Of course," cried Worplesdon, nettled at the idea that he should have omitted the obvious precaution. "And, what's more, I've seen or accounted for every arm of that sort—there aren't very many in the place—and checked it with its licence. Most of them belong to the University Revolver Club. They have a small range near the Corn Exchange. All the guns are checked by the retired sergeant, who looks after the clubroom, and put back after each practice. I'm not quite satisfied that all the members exactly keep the rules. What I mean to say is that sometimes, from what Choldcroft—that's the sergeant—says, the members do occasionally take one away for an hour or so, and that he's had the deuce of a time sometimes getting them back. But he says he's never had one missing overnight—so far as he can remember."

Bramley showed more interest than he had displayed during the conversation up to this point.

"Oh—only so far as he can remember? Are those the exact words he used?"

"Pretty near—as far as I can recall them."

The Acting Chief Constable, too, became a little more animated. It was a point to which he hadn't given much thought.

"What sort of a fellow is this Choldcroft?"

"Ordinary sort of a sergeant. What do you mean?"

"I mean—for instance—is he pretty sober?"

"In the way of alcohol, do you mean?" asked Worplesdon.

His companion nodded.

"He likes his pint, if that's what you mean. Lots of sergeants do, if it comes to that."

"Not only *Army* sergeants, either!" There was a twinkle in the big man's eyes as he spoke.

"I've often seen Sergeant Choldcroft coming out of the Wheatsheaf—as I go home after duty." He added the last words hastily. He did not wish the Scotland Yard man to think that he was accustomed to seeking the sergeant's company in a public-house after the day's work was done. "He's a man who can carry his drink, I should say."

"Never one over the eight, so far as you can say?"

Worplesdon saw the direction which Bramley's thoughts were taking.

"You mean—that there might have been times when he hadn't checked up his guns quite as carefully as he ought?"

Bramley nodded.

"You never know. Like losing the key of the office safe. Who hasn't done that some time or other—one over the eight or not? I've done it myself—in my younger days—more than once. Dare say I should now if there were one to lose. But I've got a combination safe these days—and there are one or two hidey-holes—in different places, of course—where I can pick up the letters if they go out of my mind for the time being. But what about this sergeant of yours?"

"What do you mean—what about him?" asked Worplesdon.

"Well—couldn't we get him to talk?"

The Acting Chief Constable nodded.

"I dare say. What's the time now?"

He glanced at his wrist-watch.

"Half-past six, I make it. The range closes at half-past five, on the days when it's open at all. I don't know whether to-day's one. Even if it is it's, closed by now. No use ringing up there. I don't know where Choldcroft lives. Anyway, he wouldn't be on the phone. But one of my men may know."

He was just about to press the button of the bell on his desk.

"Half a mo'," cried the other. "There's a better plan than that. Why not ring up the Wheatsheaf?"

"Do you think that's a good plan—even if he's there? Wouldn't it make him suspicious?" Worplesdon was puzzled.

"Why should it? Anyway, he'd be just as suspicious if a policeman went to fetch him from his house. And law-abiding sergeants don't like being escorted to the police station by the Force."

"All right," the Acting Chief Constable agreed. "I'll try the Wheatsheaf."

As Worplesdon got through on the telephone to the public-house, Bramley took out a small lens and, turning over the bullet in its cardboard nest, examined it again from every angle. He seemed interested in it and not satisfied with the cursory examination which he had made of it before with the naked eye. Worplesdon, as he sat with the receiver to his ear waiting for the connection to be made, eyed the London man with a slightly scornful air. He was an old-fashioned policeman: he had a healthy contempt for the scientific methods which had pervaded the Force since the days of Sherlock Holmes and all the motley band of amateur and professional detectives who had followed his footsteps, in fiction and fact, through the Edwardian period down to the neo-Georgian.

"Hullo. Oh—good evening, Mr. Candler. Worplesdon speaking. Yes—Acting Chief Constable." He was as yet unaccustomed to the exalted rank which had so recently been conferred upon him; yet he felt a certain glow of satisfaction come over him as he emphasised each syllable over the wire to the landlord. He was not unacquainted, himself, with the Wheat-sheaf's cosy bar, and he had a mental picture of the genial host holding the receiver to his ear against a background of comforting-looking bottles of various shapes and sizes with a certain air of importance, not unmixed, perhaps, with a little trepidation, as the unexpected message came over the wire from the head of the town police.

"No—we're not after *you* this time." There was a somewhat forced air in the Inspector's jocularity. "Is Sergeant Choldcroft there to-night? Or has he been in? What's that? He is? I wonder if you'd mind asking him to step round for a few minutes to see me? Yes—at the station. No—nothing very important. Shan't keep him more than a few minutes."

There was a pause during which the publican clearly passed on the summons to the keeper of the University Revolver Range.

"All right. Thanks very much."

Worplesdon hung up the receiver with relief.

"He's coming. He'll be round in a few minutes."

Glancing at the clock, Bramley checked the time, and the two men remained smoking in silence, the London man still puffing at his pipe and Worplesdon smoking a cigarette feverishly.

"Rather long minutes you have here in Cambridge?"

Bramley's tone was sarcastic as he looked at the clock and noted that a quarter of an hour had passed since his companion had passed the message over the telephone.

"Choldcroft's been having another one to keep his spirits up, I'll bet. He doesn't know what we want him for. He's a law-abiding citizen, and they're always worse than the real crooks, in my experience, when they get the police on their tracks."

But in twenty minutes the few promised ones came to an end and the orderly entered.

In order that his visitor's suspicions, if he had any, might be allayed at the outset, Bramley hastily put into his pocket the small cardboard box containing the bullet. It was just as well that his man should have no inkling as to what was to be the subject of the conversation. Unprepared witnesses were more valuable than those who had been coached, or had some idea as to what they were going to be asked. If they had time to think over the probable subject of an interview, they were more likely to colour their answers according to their own first reactions.

"Sergeant Choldcroft to see you, sir."

Choldcroft was shown in. He was very much what Bramley had pictured he would be: of medium height, with grizzled hair and a somewhat untidy moustache. His face was round, purplish and cheerful, and the Chief Inspector put him down at between fifty and sixty. He had an erect carriage, the effect of which was somewhat marred by the stomach which was beginning to make itself a prominent feature of his make-up in the ease of retirement on a pension, in a soft job, after the rigours its owner had endured in the Service.

Sergeant Choldcroft looked suspiciously from one to the other of the police officers. But his deepest mistrust was reserved for the London man, who was unknown to him.

"Sit down, Choldcroft, sit down. Let me introduce Chief Inspector Bramley—from London." He could not resist dwelling on the two last syllables, and seeing the effect they created.

Bramley's genial manner—he remembered a few good Army stories which had stood him in good stead on many a similar occasion—had its effect, and the three men were soon chatting cheerfully on any subject but that of crime.

"I'm sorry to have had to drag you all the way here, Mr. Choldcroft—Sergeant Choldcroft, I should say—but there is just a little matter on which you could, perhaps, give us some very useful information."

The Chief Inspector's tactfulness had won the day. This, combined with the extra pint or two which the visitor had obviously put down to encourage himself for the coming ordeal, had put him completely at his ease. The subject which was uppermost in Bramley's mind was broached in a tactful way.

Choldcroft was an expert on revolvers. There was just a little trouble about a certain revolver—and a bullet. Would Mr. Choldcroft—Sergeant Choldcroft—be kind enough to help them? They were themselves amateurs in such matters. The ex-sergeant began to thaw—to tell them tales of his job—of the larks which the "young gentlemen" would get up to at times; of the difficulty he sometimes had to restrain them from playing the fool with his "guns." And gradually—very gradually—as Sergeant Choldcroft became more and more confidential—the truth came out.

They were all gentlemen—all friends—that was understood. None of them would want to get either of the others into trouble. But Sergeant Choldcroft was more in need of the services of the police than he was himself. There had been a practice match—a week before—in preparation for Bisley or something. There were twenty-four revolvers belonging to the club. Fifteen had been in use that afternoon. After the practice, which lasted later than usual, Choldcroft had been persuaded by some of the young gentlemen to go round and have just one—only once in a way, of course—at the Beetle and Wedge, as some return for the extra time he had been kept and the help he had given.

"Well—you know—mates—how hard it is to refuse: they sort of get round you. To tell the truth—I did go. And, it's between friends, mind you, I did have one—had two as a matter of fact. It was a rainy day—you may remember it?—and I'd come to the range in a mack. When I went round to the Beetle and Wedge—it's only a couple of doors off the range—I didn't bother to lock the door of the place. The key was in the pocket of my mack, you see. And wrongly—quite wrongly, as I see now—I didn't take the trouble to get the key and lock the door before I went. It was only for a minute or two, and I thought I'd leave it till I locked up for the day."

And so the story rambled on, getting more and more diffuse as its point came nearer the inevitable revelation.

"And the truth of the matter is that when I *did* go back and check the revolvers—there was one missing—the usual Webley Army pattern—with the No. 16 engraved on the barrel. And from that day to this, gentlemen, try as I would, I've not been able to find it nor trace who took it. Of course, it *may* have been one of the club—though I didn't think they'd do a thing like that, that would get me into trouble. But I'm more inclined to think that it may have been someone that slipped inside when we went out. The range was empty—that I'll swear—when I left to go to the pub. The gents that didn't come with me had gone off home already."

The sergeant, having come to the point, could not get away from it, and Bramley, who had extracted as much from his witness as suited his purpose for the moment, was hard put to it to stem the tide of talk, disembarrass himself of his visitor, and have leisure to discuss the discovery with his colleague.

When, at last, in a more genial frame of mind than ever with his new-found friend, the sergeant was persuaded to go, the two policemen breathed deep sighs of relief.

"Thank God that's over. What do you say to a short visit to the Beetle and Wedge on our own account? I expect our friend will go back to the Wheatsheaf and convince the landlord that the police are his friends and not his enemies."

Worplesdon reached for his hat.

"I think we've earned one—or perhaps two."

"Passed unanimously. And I'll be staying here the night. To-morrow morning we may find the list of members of the University Revolver Club more interesting than the 'Cricket Final.'"

CHAPTER XVIII

THE REVOLVER CLUB

It was early next morning when Bramley found his way to the police station, and interrupted the Acting Chief Constable in his perusal of the list of members of the University Revolver Club which he had obtained from the secretary the night before. This told him that the membership was down to thirty-three. Sergeant Choldcroft had promised to come round during the course of the morning, to see if he were able to render any assistance in the process of going through the roll with a view to giving any useful information that he might think worth imparting to the police to aid them in their difficult researches.

"Good morning, Worplesdon."

The London man looked as fresh and cheerful as he had done the day before. He was used to mystery and puzzles and rarely allowed them to interfere with his sleep, however important the possible issue. He always maintained, with some truth, that it was not in the best interests of the public, which it was his duty as a detective to serve, to let things prey on his mind to such an extent as to interfere with his rest and render him less likely to be able to give efficient service the morning after.

Not so with Worplesdon, who was beginning to wilt under the double strain of the responsible position which had been suddenly thrust upon him, and the fresh turn which had now been given to the problem of the Cambridge murders. He looked pale and worn, and there were dark rings under his eyes.

"Before we get on with this revolver business," went on Bramley, "there's something else that I want to tell you about. I told them at the office to send on any stuff for me to the post office here, as I didn't know where I'd be off to the first thing in the morning."

He waved a bulky foolscap envelope.

"And something's come through this morning. It's not often that I'm left all alone to my own devices—or vices!" There was a twinkle in his eye as he spoke, and the local man envied the temperament which could remain consistently cheerful when such big issues were at stake.

Without saying any more for the time being the big man settled himself as comfortably as possible in the armed Windsor chair which was placed at the disposal of visitors to the Chief Constable's office and, bringing out his well-burned briar, busied himself with the important rite of filling it to the brim and over and lighting it up, allowing, at the same time, several lighted strands of tobacco to fall on the papers which he had just set down on the desk. The envelope began to smoulder.

"What a damned careless chap I am! Nearly had the whole thing up in smoke—where it'll probably end, anyway, if we aren't a bit more successful and luckier with our enquiries than we have been so far!"

He gave a full-throated laugh, and pulled a fat official letter from the envelope.

"These Colonial fellows are a bit smarter than I'd expected. They haven't had time to get a letter from here, but they've answered the cable pretty fully."

"So it seems," said Worplesdon as he eyed the voluminous document.

"And this isn't a letter. There hasn't been time for a mail to come in since the Professor was wounded. This is a copy of the cables that have been passing between West Africa and London."

Worplesdon was annoyed. He had almost forgotten the accident to Sir Wedgwood Camberley and its supposed bearing on the Cambridge tragedies. Now, when he had got a chance of going ahead with the matter of the revolver and the murder of his chief, his companion was going back a step—several steps—and reverting to a matter which, as the Acting Chief Constable conceived it, had but very little bearing on the other important matters in hand.

"And as it's from headquarters, and as they obviously think it's important, I'm bound to give it first attention. Is Choldcroft here?"

"Not yet," replied Worplesdon wearily.

"So much the better. There's plenty of time to go into the revolver matter later—and it oughtn't to take us too long."

The other was again amazed at his new friend's seeming nonchalance. In the face of what had happened on Parker's Piece only a couple of nights before he couldn't help thinking that that matter, on which Bramley had instructions to help him, should have precedence over the other. But it was of no use trying to convince Bramley.

"I don't know what it is—intuition or whatever else you like to call it. But I can't help thinking that until we get a little nearer knowing what's at the bottom of these other things that happened longer ago, we shan't make very much progress with the affair of Deepcut's death. You may say it's a silly thing for a detective to talk about intuition and such-like. But, when all's said and done, with all the science and things that we've got to help us in these days, we'd never get very far if it weren't for an occasional bright inspiration, even if it doesn't seem to have very much foundation."

What Worplesdon privately thought was that the other was just wasting words and time. Cambridge was a very pleasant place in summer, especially if you didn't have to live in it all the year round, and no doubt the London man was pleased enough to get away for a day or two from his stuffy London office. But he did not want to offend his visitor by betraying his private suspicions.

"I dare say you're right. You know better than I do. There's not much in the detective line to be done, as a rule, in a place like this, and, anyway, I don't pretend to be one; I don't belong to the local C.I.D."

Without more ado Bramley, spreading the papers before him, began to talk. Information had been cabled through from the police in Edwardsville giving the names of all Africans who had applied to the Secretariat there during the past year for passports for the voyage to England. There was a list of about fifty names, including those of Kalawa and Pompoli. The District Commissioner, young Woodward, at Mandu had, as he thought, identified the man whom the Professor had noticed in the native "barri," and who was supposed to have been guilty of the attempt to shoot Sir Wedgwood one night through the open window of the mud Rest House as he lay, half asleep, in his camp-bed, tossing and turning with discomfort in the heat to which he was by no means inured. His native name was Abu Bokari, and it was established definitely, as the Professor had written to his daughter, that he had gone to England some time in the preceding year to get commercial training in Liverpool. Scotland Yard had been in touch with the firm named in the telegrams from West Africa, and it had been established, beyond doubt, that the youth had actually reported for duty to the firm in question, and had worked with them from August till the beginning of October. He had then mysteriously disappeared. He had not proved a particularly adept pupil, taking very little interest in his work, and had often been reprimanded. The firm had, in fact, written to his father to bring the facts to his notice. Money orders in payment by instalments had been arranged with regard to his premium, and these had been received pretty punctually every fortnight. Abu Bokari had acquired a taste for dress of a kind which was too costly of one in his position, and the manager had, in a friendly way, remonstrated with the young man for the attention which he paid to a subject which had but little connection with the studies he had come to England to pursue. The youth had resented the criticism, and one day early in October had absented himself from the office. Enquiries at his lodgings had failed to disclose his whereabouts. He had, after paying his bill for a week, absconded without telling his landlady that he did not propose to return. Every police station in the country had received enquiries from Liverpool asking for reports of a negro, with a passport from Old Guinea, who had declared himself in accordance with the Aliens Act, but none that had been received disclosed the fact that Abu Bokari had made himself known.

It seemed probable that he had adopted another name and managed to efface himself in some country district where the police were not as strict as in the larger towns in enforcing the provisions of the Act.

"We had that circular here," said Worplesdon ruefully. He remembered the fruitless efforts which his staff had made, without success, to establish the identity of the young African amongst the undergraduate population of the Colleges.

"It's all very suspicious to me," said Bramley, "Here's an unaccounted African roaming the country, just about the time when two fellows from the place he comes from are bumped off in Cambridge. He turns up next in Africa, where he has a pot at the Professor whose little prejudices about blacks are bound to be known, and about whom there was a false alarm—about a gun—round about the time when these two black undergraduates were murdered. This is all just suspicion, of course. We can't definitely connect up the young man in Liverpool with the young man the Professor told his daughter he saw on the night of the murders—the young man whom your own constable saw hanging about in Brookside just after Kalawa had been done in. But it's more than just odd that he's supposed to have been seen again at Mandu, and only a short time before the Professor himself was shot at and nearly murdered."

Worplesdon admitted that it was odd: it was difficult for anyone not to do so. But it all seemed to him a fantastic jumble of guessing and filling up imaginary clues: not at all like the steady, solid police work that he had himself been used to.

"But what's all this got to do with the bullet that young Cranston found in the punt yesterday? And what has it got to do with the revolver club that we sent for Choldcroft about yesterday?"

"Ask me another," said Bramley blandly. "I don't know, any more than you. But it's my job, your job, to try to make some sort of sense out of this jigsaw, if it can be done. And there's no reason why it shouldn't, so far as I can see. It's more than mere coincidence, must be, that this sudden crime wave should come on in Cambridge, and reach out to Africa, where Professor Camberley, from Cambridge, happens to be. And from what you and others have told me of Sir Wedgwood, he doesn't seem, with all his eccentricities, to be the sort of man who just imagines things. You've seen the copy of the letter that he sent to his daughter—that the young lady herself sent to you and to us. It's mighty queer that he—who'd never been to Africa before, in a place where, so they tell me, to a newcomer all coons look alike—should spot this fellow in the 'barri,' or whatever they call it, and immediately connect him up with the man he saw that night in Brookside—just before Kalawa got what was coming to him."

"Well, it's all very puzzling," said Worplesdon, whose looks were in keeping with his words. "But don't forget that Choldcroft is due here any minute, and we've got to keep our minds on this revolver business and the bullet in the punt."

Bramley accepted the rebuke gracefully. His thoughts had been running away with him, and he had worked rather farther from the business of the morning than he had intended.

"Of course—of course. Only I've got it so firmly fixed in my mind that we shall find, in the end, that all these things are somehow connected up together that I look at the thing as a whole—or rather, I look on all the jig-saw bits as parts that will one day, when we get on the track of the solution, make up a coherent story."

The orderly entered.

"Mr. Choldcroft to see you."

Worplesdon, having asked the London man if he were ready, said he would see the sergeant.

"Good morning, sir—good morning, Worplesdon." The sergeant distinguished the London visitor from the local police chief by his mode of address, which he was not displeased to see the Acting Chief Constable distinctly resented. Choldcroft was on his dignity this morning. The message which he had received from the constable sent by Worplesdon had been a little curt, and he was resolved to have a little of his own back.

"Sit down, Choldcroft," retorted Worplesdon, who knew that his visitor did not mind whether the prefix to his name was mister or sergeant, but who objected to the bare appellation itself except from his bosom cronies. And the Acting Chief Constable had not been initiated into the magic circle.

"Good morning, sergeant," cried Bramley more tactfully. "We're depending on you a lot this morning about this revolver business."

The ex-sergeant positively purred.

"Anything that I can do—I shall only be too happy. I've been a Government man myself—am still, in a manner of speaking, as I'm drawing a pension, as you might say."

Bramley produced from his pocket the list of members of the University Revolver Club.

"Of course, sergeant, this means very little to us, without your help. Smith of Corpus and Jones of Trinity are one and the same to us. But you ought to be able to put us on the track of something that might help us."

Sergeant Choldcroft oozed self-importance, but modestly deprecated the usefulness of his own possible contribution to the work of the police. He was also aware of a certain feeling of guilt. Had he not had the lapse to which he had confessed the previous night, the work of the police might not have been complicated by the search for the man who had taken the revolver. And in the cold light of the morning, without the supporting stimulus of a couple of pints of the Wheat-sheaf's best, he did not feel quite the same confidence in the presence of the officers of the law as he had done the night before. But Bramley seemed friendly enough. He wouldn't do himself any good by trying to obstruct the Scotland Yard detective.

"You just tell me what you want—how you think I can help—and I'm your man."

There was no use beating about the bush any longer.

"It is very important, sergeant, for us to trace the fellow who got away with that revolver—No. 16. Have you any sort of idea, any kind of suspicion, whom it might have been?"

Sergeant Choldcroft looked alarmed. Was his transgression at length to be publicly unmasked? So far he had managed to evade any unpleasant consequences of his act of omission. Given time, and tact, with some judicious questioning of the young gentlemen who were members of the club, he might be able to coax out of them who had been responsible for the abstraction. Unless—and his blood ran cold within him as he realised the implication of his thoughts—the fellow who had taken it had removed it for some felonious purpose: unless, indeed, he were actually the man who had murdered the Chief Constable two nights ago on Parker's Piece. Not until then had the full possible consequences of his peccadillo dawned upon him. And here he was, in the presence, not merely of the Acting Chief Constable, but also of a well-known Chief Inspector from Scotland Yard, whose business it was to rout out every detail in connection with the crime, without fear or favour, and recking nothing of the consequences to any witness who might be involved, so long as he achieved his object—the tracking of the man who was responsible for the crime.

He was indeed on the horns of a dilemma. If he showed unwillingness to assist when asked to do so voluntarily, their suspicions might fasten themselves upon him. He might be viewed in the light of an accessory before or after the fact, whatever the legal term might be. If he submitted to their questions, the truth which came out might be equally damaging to him. Brought before a court on subpœna, he might be cross-examined in public and, as the result of the admissions he might be forced to make, be compelled to disclose his negligence in public, and so lose the post which so comfortably eked out his exiguous Army pension.

He determined to be as obliging and useful as possible this morning. If he managed to please Bramley, it was possible that worse consequences might be averted and his share in the tracing of the murderer, if it came to that, be veiled in the decent obscurity of the police's secret archives. He scratched his head and pulled nervously at his untidy moustache. The licensed houses weren't open at this hour (how much better they managed these things in Flanders, where the *estaminets* were open at all sorts of hours night and day). But he might have braced himself a little for the ordeal which he might have known was before him by a timely nip or two at the brandy flask which he kept at home "in case of illness." However, it was no use crying over spilt milk. He must keep up his end as well as he could without the use of artificial stimulants.

"There were a lot of members there that day—seeing that the team was more or less being chosen."

This was hedging, as he knew, though it was true. But he wanted to try to discover, if possible, on what lines the detective's mind was working.

"You mean you would find it difficult to remember who was actually there?"

Choldcroft nodded.

"Except the four or five young gentlemen who took me to the Beetle and Wedge."

Perhaps his statement would be accepted and he would be pressed no further. But his hopes were dashed by Bramley's next question.

"But there aren't much more than thirty in the club, all told, if the list's correct. I don't suppose the whole lot were there?"

"No—they weren't. That I *do* remember." Then, with a sigh, as he passed his hand in a puzzled manner over his brow and saw that he must go through with it: "I think," he said, "I might be able to recollect some of them."

Bramley took out a pencil and made ready to tick off on the list before him the names which the sergeant might mention. The names of the five who had escorted him to the public-house were Horsell and Grimbly, of St. John's, Westfield and Newton, of Trinity, and Peters, of Caius. Charlecote, of Sidney, the running Blue, had come along with the others, but had left them at the door of the Beetle and Wedge. By dint of hard thinking he was able to recall the names of six more men: Travers, of Peterhouse,

Flinders, Smith and Harper, of Selwyn, and a Frenchman from Downing whose name he could not pronounce, but which he believed to be something like Dupont (pronounced phonetically). Cudgel his brains as he would he could remember no more, and Bramley checked up the list with his pencil.

"That makes a dozen. You can't think of any more?"

"No—I'm afraid I can't."

Choldcroft was quite positive.

"That's a pretty good turn-up—for the summer term. I'm pretty sure I've got them all at last." He breathed a sigh of relief.

There was a knock at the door. The orderly came in with some letters and a parcel which he placed on Worplesdon's desk.

"Hullo—your birthday?" said Bramley, eyeing the package, and inclined to relax now that he had got some sort of information on which he might begin an investigation.

"Not me," said Worplesdon. He glanced at the postmark on the parcel, which seemed to contain a box about the size of an ordinary boot-box. "Something from London—official, I expect. I don't have my private things sent here to the station."

He brought out a penknife and cut the string, and began to unwrap the brown paper which enclosed it.

"Well, Mr. Choldcroft, I don't think we need bother you yet awhile. Where can I get the addresses of these young men? I may have to interview them all."

Choldcroft's heart sank again. He would eventually be brought still farther into the matter: his worst fears were being realised.

"It only gives their Colleges. But there's a list of lodgings published by the University. I've got one at home: I'll look them up for you."

He was about to take his leave when the Acting Chief Constable, who had taken off the lid of the box, drew out a heavy-looking object wrapped in tissue-paper and began to strip it of its covering.

"Might be a bomb or something; better be careful," said Bramley flippantly. To his astonishment Worplesdon gave a cry of amazement, and dropped the object on the floor.

"My God!" he cried.

Bramley and Choldcroft looked to see what had elicited his ejaculation. And when they saw the cause of it, they uttered similar remarks.

For the thing which the parcel had contained was an Army pattern Webley revolver.

CHAPTER XIX

THE AVENGER

"I AM perfectly all right, I assure you."

Sir Wedgwood Camberley's tone was firm enough. But his pale face, and the dark hollows under his eyes, belied his words.

"I came out here, at the instance of the University, to do certain work. It is my duty not to return until that work is completed. The wound is quite healed—the doctor says so—and I shall do myself more harm than good by lying up here any longer, besides being a nuisance to you and to everybody else who has been so kind to me."

Woodward, the District Commissioner, saw that it was useless to try any further to coax his guest to give up the expedition and return to England. And he admired the Professor for his spirit, much as he feared that his presence would be an embarrassment in his District. He felt personally, as well as officially, responsible for the safety of the Government's guest, and he had determined not to allow him to travel farther into the interior of the country without a good-sized escort. His own police force was much depleted, as the Provincial Commissioner, who was engaged upon settling a dispute between a Chief from one of the neighbouring Districts and one from his own, had drawn heavily upon his detachment for his own purposes and for keeping order during the meetings between the Chiefs, when feeling ran high and there was always the possibility of a disturbance.

"I have scarcely begun the work I set myself out to do. I cannot begin to execute a proper anthropological survey of these tribes and peoples until I have been able to give some time to the study of the country where they live and the conditions under which they exist. That I can only do—and you agreed with me on this point in our earlier discussions on the subject—when I have stayed with them in at least a dozen of their villages and, with the help of the interpreter you have kindly placed at my disposal, had a good many interviews with people of different types and callings at the various places I shall include in my itinerary."

Even as he spoke the Professor burst into a paroxysm of coughing. The wound which he had received that night in the Rest House, as he lay asleep in his camp-bed, had fortunately been a slight one. But it had caused a certain amount of damage to his lung. At home, in Europe, the odds were that it would mend very quickly. But conditions in West Africa, especially in the bush, where Sir Wedgwood was proposing to spend the next month or more, are hardly the same. Skilled nursing and attention were out of the question. Whilst he remained at Mandu, the District Commissioner's station, he had been able to receive the attentions of the District doctor; he had been put up in Woodward's own European-built concrete bungalow; and a certain degree of comfort could be obtained. The young man saw that, were he to have any chance of breaking down the Professor's resolve, he would have to adopt other tactics.

"Whilst you were lying ill, sir, I did not like to trouble you with a lot of things that might have interfered in any way with your recovery. But there have been developments of which I think I ought to tell you now. I don't think—nobody thinks—for a moment that the man who tried to get you that night was a common or garden thief. Thieves in this country don't use guns when they are at their work. They want to try to do the job unnoticed and, if they are not successful, to be able to fade away with as little attention attracted to themselves as possible. In any case, there wasn't any need to shoot if the fellow was just after pinching some of your stuff. Your hut was open, and the policeman on duty on the veranda—although he denies it, of course—was certainly asleep: they always are. And the fellow who tried to murder you—for that was certainly his object—would know that well enough. If he just wanted to steal your property, what need was there for him to take aim through the open window at you as you lay in bed? There would be no point in it at all. Even the bush natives here don't do silly things like that. Nothing was stolen; we know that. If he'd pinched something, and then you had been awakened, there would be just the possibility of his having a shot at you to prevent your giving the alarm. But what really happened? The shot he fired actually gave the alarm: woke up the policeman, and brought me and more of the men running to find out what had been happening."

The Professor, propped up with cushions at his back in the long Madeira chair on the District Commissioner's veranda, listened in obstinate silence. He didn't like being talked to like that by a young man. Though he felt inwardly bound to admit that this young man was talking what seemed, in the cold light of reason, good enough sense.

"When you told me about the man you had seen in the 'barri'—the man who reminded you of someone you had seen in Cambridge on the night that the two niggers were murdered—I had enquiries made. My constables know the man: we know that he went to England last year, and the police at home have been on his track. He changed his name after he left Liverpool, and there is no news yet how he managed to leave the country and get back here. These people are just as good as anyone else at faking passports, and that would probably not have been difficult. They aren't so smart at enquiring into them now that the war is over. Anyway, as no trace has been found of the man by the police in England, it's a possible assumption that he did find his way back here. He may have landed at a French port—or in Liberia—and got back to Old Guinea over the border. There's lots of trouble in that way over smuggling spirits and getting unlicensed guns into the country."

He paused for a moment to see the effect of his words on his listener. Sir Wedgwood, who had listened intently to the recital, gave no outward clue to his inward reactions.

"You won't, of course, forget that you have actually met the father of one of the fellows who was murdered. These people, like all country people all over the world, gossip and talk like the deuce. Rather more than many, in fact. They can't read or write, so they can only get their information by word of mouth. And you know the game called 'Russian Scandal' that they used to play at parties at home. You know how a story grows, like a snowball, when it is passed from mouth to mouth, from people of different intelligence and powers of observation to each other. You have never disguised your feelings about what you think—and many others think—to be the inadvisability of the coloured races going to a home university for their education. These people would jump to the conclusion that you hated their race just because it *was* their race."

Sir Wedgwood smiled indulgently. This young man, his host, was making as good a case as he could for his theory. He would pride himself, of course, that he knew the natives of the country better than his guest. That was a debatable point. The Professor had spent the greater part of his life in studying anthropology—with special reference to the negro races. He was likely to know at least as much as a youth who had only spent a year or so in Africa, doing administrative work at that, and knowing, even if it were by practical experience, an infinitesimal part of the great continent to which he had been posted. It was a great pity that he had ever mentioned his suspicion to Woodward that the man he had seen in the "barri" that morning bore any resemblance to the one he had seen near Brookside in the winter term at Cambridge. His reference to that matter, which was still fresh in the minds of the public, and revived from time to time by the Press when they were hard pressed for other sensational news, had suggested all kinds of further theories to his young host. But he did not like to check the obviously genuine enthusiasm of the District Commissioner.

"Then your theory," he said, "amounts to this. That the people out here, including the father of Kalawa, believe that I am so prejudiced against their race that I went so far as to murder at least one native from Old Guinea who offended my sense of what was proper by going as an undergraduate to Cambridge?"

He smiled, and waited for a reply.

"I know it sounds ridiculous to you; but lots of things can happen out here that anyone who had never been here before would never believe possible. Look at the Human Leopard Society. The people—some of them—firmly believe that certain people can change themselves into leopards and murder their enemies whilst they are changed in that way. I've had some of these cases to deal with and, believe me, they are carried out in such a way that though I won't say I've been near believing it myself, I can easily see how uneducated, illiterate, superstitious people can get the idea fixed in their heads. Surely people who can convince themselves that leopard murders can take place would find very little difficulty in thinking an Englishman who hated negroes was capable of carrying his dislike to the extent of committing murder when he had the objects of his hatred in his power in his own country?"

The Professor would not be convinced; and thinking the matter over again in the cold light of reason, Woodward was not surprised at his reluctance to accept his theory as a fact.

"I see, from the Reuter which you were kind enough to lend me this morning, that the Chief Constable of Cambridge has been found dead—apparently murdered—and with a revolver—on Parker's Piece. Are you going to connect that up with me, too? It would seem just as likely to me as to try to make out that the attack made on me on the Rest House here had anything to do with my views on the acceptance of negroes as students at Cambridge or Oxford!"

His host did not reply for a moment. He didn't quite know what to think. Before ever he came to the Coast, he had been told all sorts of stories about native secret societies, their ramifications and their power. But he had always understood that they operated amongst the people themselves. So far as he knew no white man had been the object of their machinations. But the attack on the Professor, and the train of thought that it had set up in connection with the Cambridge murders, had somewhat shaken his former ideas. Whilst the people of the country were outside the sphere of European influence, whilst they looked upon the white man as a sort of god, it was not to be expected that they would dare to employ against him the wiles which they used against each other. But the African had made progress in many branches of learning, especially in the past few years and during the war, when African troops had been brought into close contact with their white confrères. There were Africans to be found in every department of the Government of the Colony, technical, financial, administrative and otherwise, and black men were easily to be found who were as well versed in radio and wireless as any men in similar positions at home. They could run railway engines, repair cars, practise as doctors, act in the courts as solicitors and barristers, and there were even African stipendiary magistrates in many of the country courts. It did not need a great stretch of the imagination to envisage some of the more enterprising amongst them deciding to employ their own peculiar methods of revenge and punishment against white men who, for one reason or another, should be deemed fit to suffer.

"I know, sir," said the District Commissioner at last, "that you'll think I'm very foolish. But—leaving out for the time being the case of the murdered Chief Constable—which may or may not have some connection with the other affairs—I would not at once rule out the idea that there's something behind all this that may link up the attack on you, and the murders of Kalawa and Pompoli, in some sort of way that we haven't been able to hit upon yet. You may, of course, argue that natives who are advanced enough to be able to acquire the benefits of a European education, and learn all about science and machinery and things that are so far removed from their own daily life, would, at the same time, drop all their old superstitions and things. But there are cases that prove—fairly recent cases—that that isn't what always happens. There was a case in a West African Colony, not so very long ago, that I've read about, where a lot of mysterious leopard crimes—murders committed by the Human Leopard Society—took place.

And when the matter was enquired into and the whole case properly thrashed out in Court by people who knew the sort of thing they were dealing with, the man who was found to be at the bottom of the trouble—the instigator of the whole affair—was the son of a Chief who had been educated by some Americans as a Christian when he was a boy. He was even taken over to the States, took a degree in theology at some University over there, and even assumed Holy orders. He came back to Africa when his studies were finished. His father, the Chief, died not very long after, and the negro son, who had become a parson, and was working in his own Chiefdom as a missionary, was elected Chief in his stead. He cancelled his orders—or whatever one does to stop being a minister—and became the ruler of the country. In spite of all his training and education, his ancestry—or whatever you like to call it—was too much for him. He was won over by the members of the Leopard Society to which his family had belonged, dabbled in all sorts of horrible crime and murder, and was caught out. They weren't able to bring any of the actual murders quite home to him. But the evidence of his complicity was so strong that they were able to detain him on some sort of charge and pass sentence of exile. He may, if he's still alive, still be there for all I know."

The Professor, who had listened without interruption whilst his host was speaking, cleared his throat and took a sip at the lime drink by his side. He nodded slowly.

"I've heard something of the case myself: I came across it in the course of my investigations on another matter. But I don't quite see how it fits in here. There would be some point in it, I admit, *if* it had been in America that the young man had redeveloped the cannibalistic instincts of his forefathers and started to commit murders actually in the United States. But he didn't. It wasn't till he got back to Africa—*in his own native environment*—that the blood lust, or whatever you choose to call it, overcame him. I can quite understand it. In this case the murders took place in England. It is true that, owing to the officiousness of the police about a revolver for which I had omitted to take out a licence, my name was brought by local gossip into prominence soon after the occurrences. It is true, also, that I had made no secret of my views on the unsuitability of Cambridge University as a place where Africans—or any other coloured people for that matter—should be trained and educated. But is it likely that a man like your friend from Sierra Leone—for that is where the incidents you refer to occurred—having acquired a high degree of knowledge and training and intimacy with white men's affairs, would be such a simpleton as to believe such rumours and stories as were circulated about me?"

The District Commissioner shook his head dubiously.

"I've not been very long in the service; and I say, quite candidly, that I don't understand the working of the native mind, and what's more, I don't believe that any other white man does, or will."

"I think," said Sir Wedgwood, "that you go rather far. If what you say is true, then the whole of my lifework, the very reason for my venturing to this country at all, is of no account. No, sir, I have put my hand to the plough and I must go through with it. If your suspicions are correct, I must, as it were, use myself as a bait. If the attack on me was based on such motives as you suggest, there is all the more reason why I should stay. Subsequent events may prove the truth of it or otherwise. If things should be at all as you say and think, and we can definitely establish your hypothesis, consider what a valuable starting-point we shall have secured for further investigations on the same lines." The Professor smiled enigmatically. "We may even," he continued slowly, "stumble, out here, on the solution of the mystery of the Cambridge murders."

Young Woodward saw that it was useless to reason with his guest. The most that he could do, in his effort to secure his departure home, or to the comparative safety of the capital of the Colony, was to send a confidential report to the Colonial Secretary in the hope that the authorities would take the necessary action to convince the Professor of the futility and even the personal danger of his further prolonging his stay in a District where feeling against him, owing to the recent visit amongst the people of the father of the undergraduate Pompoli, who had met his death in his College rooms in the University town, ran high.

"Well, sir, it's late, and I must be getting along to the office. If I can't persuade you to change your mind, I shall have to order your carriers. They are a bit difficult to get at this time of the year, when the people are looking after their rice crops—especially as you need so many. But I will see what I can do."

Sir Wedgwood thanked the District Commissioner. He had gained his point: there would be no further opposition from this young man, who ruled the District, but who must be made to see that the claims of science must be acknowledged before those of the ordinary everyday administrative duties.

Woodward picked up his topee, and was about to open the front door which led to the flight of steps from the bungalow floor to the ground, when there was a knock on the door.

In answer to Woodward's shout the door was opened, and a smart constable entered and, saluting heavily with a stamp of his bare foot on the polished wooden floor, handed the Commissioner a letter.

"Na letter, sah—for the Professor."

The District Commissioner took the envelope from the man and, as he handed it to his guest, noted that it was registered and that the address was written in untidy block capitals.

"How you get this letter? Which persin go sign for it?"

"The Chief Clerk, sah. The letter done come from the post office in your bag, sah."

The Commissioner dismissed the orderly, and was about to follow him out down the steps.

"Wait a minute, please, Woodward."

The Professor had opened the envelope and was reading the contents of the letter within with obvious interest. The young man noted that his hand was shaking. The Commissioner stood for a minute or two till Sir Wedgwood came to the end of his perusal. Then, with a short, dry laugh, the Professor handed it to him.

"Ha! Read that. A practical joke, I should think. I hope you haven't taken an indirect way of trying to scare me off."

The Professor tried to infuse a mocking tone into his words, but a glance was sufficient to tell his host that he was moved.

Woodward put down his helmet, took up the sheet of paper and, sitting down in the chair which he had just left, began to read.

It was a soiled piece of lined foolscap, jagged at one corner as if torn from its companion sheet by a clumsy hand. The writing on the paper was in faded cheap brown ink, and was all in laboriously made and imperfectly formed block capitals.

"Mandu.

"June 15th, 1935.

"SIR,

"You have escaped us once. We are more than one: we are many. The Chief, Brima, is not responsible for what we do. He does not know that we are working to avenge his son. But he knows, as we all do, that, even if you did not yourself kill his son, Pompoli, and Ogu Kalawa too, in England, we have read it in the English papers, and we have heard what other white men say, that you are not friend to black man. You want to drive them *all* from your country. Pompoli—and Kalawa—would not go. They were scholars; they wanted to learn English book. That was why, at their fathers' expense, they went to Cambridge College. But you hated them: you wanted to kill them. Even if you did not, as we say, kill them yourself, you were behind the people who did the thing. We know: one of us watched you on the night that Pompoli was killed. You were near—you know it—everybody knows it. Even if you did not do the murder yourself, you *knew* who did it—and you did nothing to help the young man when he was attacked. Of course not: you wanted him to die. You come to black man's country: you think because you are white, and all white men know you, and the Government protects you, that you will be safe. You have escaped once, because we were not careful in what we did. YOU WILL NOT ESCAPE AGAIN. Go—*now*—if you want to see Cambridge again.

"THE BAD CROWD."

CHAPTER XX

A FRESH SCENT

THE arrival of the mysterious package containing the Webley revolver had not made things any easier for Worplesdon and the man from London. Sergeant Choldcroft, after a short examination, had affirmed that it was, without doubt, the missing arm from the University range. He had shown the police officers the number 16 plainly engraved on the barrel. And to make the identification complete, there was a miniature replica of the arms of the University stamped clearly on the butt.

"I suppose we ought to examine it for fingerprints?"

Chief Inspector Bramley nodded.

"Not that I think that's going to lead us anywhere. You can see that the thing has been all cleaned and polished up before it was posted."

Using a sheet of his morning paper, he carefully lifted up the weapon to examine it further. Whilst he did so Worplesdon shook out the box to make sure that there was nothing in it that would give a clue to the identity of the sender. But he found nothing but a large quantity of tissue-paper in which the weapon had been wrapped, and which was packed so tightly around it that it could not rattle or move in its container.

Bramley shook his head.

"The thing's been very carefully cleaned. I don't suppose, sergeant, that you could have made a better job of it yourself?"

Sergeant Choldcroft shook his head. It was, in fact, cleaned a good deal more thoroughly than he had ever cleaned it himself.

"Of course," went on the London detective, "just because it looks so spick and span, it doesn't mean that there *mightn't* be marks on it still that would come up under the powder. But I'm afraid that whoever sent it knew what he was up to. He's cleaned it deliberately in case there *should* be any clue to implicate him."

"But what the deuce can he mean by sending it to us—to the police? Must be a damned fool, I should say. An escaped lunatic, perhaps." The Chief Constable was terse.

Again Bramley disagreed.

"I think, myself, that it's a very clever move. The fellow who used this thing, as we must conjecture for a start, to kill poor Deepcut knew quite well the difficulty that criminals often do have in getting away with the instrument they have used to commit crimes. Rivers can be dragged: dust destructors have often yielded up valuable clues which have led to the discovery of more than one murderer who lived long enough to learn that you can be a bit too clever. I think myself that, if this thing was sent to you by the fellow who did the Chief Constable in, it's a very smart piece of work. I suppose every murderer who's used a weapon of some sort to do the crime is always nervous that the thing he used, if it comes at the wrong time into the hands of the police, may give him away and put the rope round his neck. I can't think of a better way myself of certainly disposing of the evidence than to put it, made harmless by having the fingerprints that might be on it removed, straight into the hands of the fellows who're to chase him before they've had time to get really busy."

"I never thought of it like that," said Worplesdon, and the unfortunate Sergeant Choldcroft looked thoroughly unhappy. He was thinking more of the consequences to himself when his laxity came to be known, as it was now almost bound to do, than of the dire results which his negligence had had in the case of the Chief Constable of Cambridge. He didn't see that there was very much chance of his keeping his job unless he managed to do some useful work in assisting the regular police to run the criminal to earth. And his face, as Bramley looked at him, lit up by the bright rays of the morning sun streaming through the office window, betrayed anything but astuteness and intelligence.

"It came from London, you say?" said Bramley. "What office was it posted at?"

Worplesdon examined the label which had been attached to the string securing the sinister package.

"The West Central Office: that's in Holborn."

From the tone in which he added the last three words a listener would have sensed that he considered this a brilliant piece of deduction.

"How's it addressed? Typed, or what?" asked Bramley.

"It's done in ink—in block capitals." He handed the label to the Chief Inspector.

"H'm. Doesn't give us too much to go on." He eyed Choldcroft. "Thank you, Mr.—Sergeant Choldcroft. I think you might go and have a preliminary run round these fellows who were at the range that day." He thought that, in his own interest, the sergeant would execute this commission to the best of his ability. And it might be better that the job should be done, in the first instance, by a civilian, and a man who had a right, by virtue of his office, to make such enquiries. The guilty man, in the very unlikely event of his being amongst the dozen undergraduates who had been using the range that day, and had accompanied the sergeant to the public-house, would be less likely to be suspicious of him than of a police officer.

So Choldcroft, perspiring profusely, took his leave, and eagerly agreed to fall in with Bramley's suggestion.

"I doubt if he'll be able to do much. But I think that we'd better do our further consulting about this case without him. He's pretty certain to pay a visit to the Wheatsheaf as soon as it opens. He'll feel the need of a stimulant. And beer, like wine, openeth the heart of man, and all kinds of gossip will be round the town before we know where we are."

Worplesdon agreed.

"He's gas-bag enough—in the ordinary way—even without the assistance of a couple of pints—or three."

"The obvious thing to do," said Bramley, putting down the label and pulling out his pipe, "is to get in touch with the railway staff—especially the men on duty when the early trains leave in the morning. They're more likely to have noticed something than the staff at the West Central Post Office. Parcels aren't accepted after a certain time. The fellow who was cute enough to think of sending this gun straight to the police station would have savvy enough not to take it to the post office when there were only a few customers about. If my theory is right, he'd have the sense to go to the place when it was full of clerks buying stamps, people sending wires, paying telephone accounts and putting deposits in the Savings Bank. Of course, he could have gone to a post office near King's Cross or Liverpool Street. If he were a nervous sort of fellow, he would have done: he'd naturally want to get rid of the thing as quick as he could. But he's not nervous. He's got his wits about him. So he goes to a place sufficiently far from the railway stations to draw another red herring across his trail. No—we've got a cool-headed customer to deal with, and we shall want all the wits we can spare."

It all sounded so delightfully easy to Worplesdon now that the big man traced out his own theory of what had happened to the man who murdered Deepcut, and the way he had disposed of the evidence of his crime. He wasn't himself much use at detective work: it had never been in his line.

"The writing doesn't help us any—on the face of it."

He took another look at the label. Whilst he was doing so there was a peal on the telephone bell, and Worplesdon, with a weary air, took up the receiver.

"Hallo. Yes—speaking. Oh, good morning, Mr. Knight. Yes—yes. Certainly: come round at once. There's an officer from Scotland Yard with me now. Yes—come right along."

He put down the receiver, and in a worried tone addressed his companion.

"It's Knight—Archer Knight—the editor of the *Cambridge Daily*

Echo. Says he's got something that will interest us. Said the best thing he could do would be to come round and show it me himself. He sounded all het up."

"Good, good," said Bramley, rubbing his hands together and puffing deeply at his pipe which was going strongly now, rather more strongly than Worplesdon, who was a confirmed cigarette smoker, liked. "The more I can get through while I'm here the better. There's nothing much we can do till he does come. What about putting something on the three-thirty?" He picked up part of the paper which was still intact after his handling of the revolver. "I expect you know a bookie not too far off?"

Worplesdon nodded ruefully.

"I know a good many—too many. They're not too friendly with me. There aren't many of them hereabouts that I haven't pinched one time or another. I've had a damned sight more money out of them—one way and another, than they've ever had out of me or are likely to."

To his great relief the court officer came in to discuss a few points in connection with the charge sheet for the police court which was sitting that morning. Bramley was disappointed at not being able to have something on; but he solaced himself whilst the Chief Constable was engaged with the sergeant by studying the "form" described by his pet racing prophet in the columns of his newspaper. As soon almost as the business was finished the editor was announced.

Archer Knight was a keen-faced, youngish man, tall and alert and with the eyes of a journalist, which seemed to take in at once every detail of his surroundings. But he was not out for 'copy' this morning: he had come to supply it. The introduction to the stranger over, he plunged straight into his business.

"I know what nailers you are for finger-prints and all that. I dare say this envelope has enough already all over it from sorters and postmen and what not. But you can never be too careful: all good editors know that!"

He gave a short laugh, and produced from his pocket a large envelope from which he shook another on to the table.

"I've got something which may or may not interest you. It wouldn't be the first time somebody had tried to play a practical joke on me. Editors and such-like are fair game—always. Just have a look at that."

His words were addressed to the Acting Chief Constable. But Worplesdon inclined his head in Bramley's direction.

"I think," said he, "you'd better let Mr. Bramley have it. He's more used to this sort of thing than I."

Eagerly Bramley, his hands protected by a piece of the prophet's most prophetic page, took up the smaller envelope and drew out what looked like a piece of ruled paper torn from a child's exercise book.

"Read that," said Knight, with more excitement in his tone than an editor usually permits himself to display.

And Bramley read out from the paper he held.

"It's in block capitals again," said Bramley, for his colleague's benefit, "and it's addressed to the editor of the *Cambridge Daily Echo*. Hullo—there's a postal order here too—for ten shillings, not made out to anybody. It was issued yesterday, at the Gray's Inn Road Post Office."

Worplesdon began to show a livelier interest.

"'Please insert the following in an early issue. I enclose P.O. for 10s., which I estimate will cover cost.'" Bramley read out the message slowly so that his hearers could follow.

And this was the text of the advertisement which the anonymous writer—unaware apparently of the newspaper rule which requires a name and address—wished the editor to publish:

"TO ALL WHOM IT MAY CONCERN (and to police officers in particular)—TAKE NOTICE THAT IN FUTURE ALL COLOURED -STUDENTS WHO SEEK TO JOIN AN ENGLISH UNIVERSITY DO SO AT THEIR PERIL. POLICE OFFICERS AND OTHERS WHO AID AND ABET SUCH STUDENTS OR TRY TO ELUCIDATE THE MYSTERIES OF THEIR SUDDEN DEATHS SHOULD REALISE WHAT IS COMING TO THEM. WE ARE JUST—WE ARE POWERFUL—WE ARE INVISIBLE.

"THE WORSE CROWD."

Worplesdon put down the cigarette which the editor had offered him unlighted. He gazed dumbly first at Bramley and then at Knight.

The Chief Inspector replaced the scrap of paper on the desk before him. "Well, I'll be *damned*."

CHAPTER XXI

THE MISSING LINK?

DURING the next day or two the Acting Chief Constable had no reason to complain of stagnation. He had begun to think, as almost everyone else in the town, and everyone throughout the country who followed the courses of mysterious crimes had begun to think, that the two strange murders of coloured undergraduates would have to be relegated to the ever-growing list of crimes of which the police had to confess they were unable to find an explanation.

The murder of his superior officer, the strange disappearance of the club revolver, the still stranger circumstances which surrounded its return and, finally, the enigmatic advertisement which had been shown them by the editor of the newspaper, all tended to convince him that their work on the previous crimes had merely been interrupted. There was no knowing to what lengths the thing might go if effective action were not taken at once.

Bramley had been inclined to put down the murders to the action of a lunatic. But events tended to show that the madman, if the criminal were one, had some sort of purpose in his fatal work. If, as the newspaper advertisement—if it were not a hoax, a possibility which always had to be considered, especially in the University town—showed, the murderer's purpose in committing the murders had some sort of justification, from his point of view, in keeping the English Universities free from the infusion of coloured blood, and if he were one and the same person who had got hold of the club revolver and used it with such deadly effect against the Chief Constable, it looked as if he had stumbled upon some suspicion that the police had got upon his track.

Bramley and Worplesdon, by the most diligent searching of the late Chief Constable's official confidential files and semi-official note-books, could find no sort of basis for such a theory. As far as they were able to ascertain, as much from documents found after his death as from statements which he was known to have made before, that was far from being the truth. The murder of Deepcut, viewed from this angle, seemed to have no sort of rhyme or reason.

Then there were those strange happenings reported from Africa—the apparently unprovoked attack upon Sir Wedgwood Camberley which had so nearly put an end to the distinguished Professor's career, and the anonymous letter which he had recently received, the text of which had been fully cabled in code to Scotland Yard.

Choldcroft's enquiries into the disappearance of the revolver had had some result, but not one which seemed likely to prove of very much use in tracing the person who had eventually put it to so tragic a use. It seemed pretty clear to him that none of the young men who had accompanied him to the Wheatsheaf could have been responsible for its disappearance. The weapon was bulky, and he would have noticed it had it been carried to the public-house by one of the party. When the mild carouse was over, he had bidden the young men good-bye on the threshold of the inn, and none of them had followed him when he went to secure the premises before returning home. This whittled the enquiry down to an examination of the six other undergraduates who had been firing that afternoon, but who had not accompanied the rest to the Wheatsheaf. He had visited each of them in turn. He had taken the line of appealing to their good nature and sense of honour not to let him down in his dilemma. It would have been bad enough at any other time for his shirking of his obvious duty—to secure the weapons in his charge and the range before indulging his private pleasures—to come out. It was a thousand times worse when, close upon the fact of this remissness, came the news of the death of the Chief Constable of the town as the result of a wound from a Webley revolver which had subsequently been unquestionably identified with the one which should have been safely in his charge.

Much to his relief he had found all the young men quite ready to help him. The possibility of a small fine as the punishment of a foolish prank was as nothing to the graver one that the course of justice, and in a case of murder at that, might be hindered by any attempt to conceal the peccadillo. It was not until, with endless difficulty, he had, in the course of one morning, traced the fourth man on his list that he had any indication of success. It was in the rooms of Bernard Travers, of Peterhouse, that he at length made a lucky hit. Travers was a freshman of the previous October term who was, whether by coincidence or not it was impossible to state at once, destined for the West African Civil Service. He admitted, almost as soon as the sergeant had made known the object of his quest, that it was he who, in a foolish moment, had taken home the revolver, No. 16, which he had been using on the range that afternoon, to his rooms in College. His explanation, one which might be considered lame enough, was that, as the Mays were shortly coming on, he would be able to use it, with blank cartridges, to excellent effect to urge on the second Peterhouse boat, which was reputed to have the chance of making its four bumps. As the revolver shoot which he had attended that afternoon was to be the last until the racing was over, he had not anticipated that his abstraction would be noticed until he had had time to replace the weapon at the next meeting due to be held.

Bramley had questioned the ingenuousness of this explanation. Whether there were to be another meeting in the near future or not, the young man must have known that the sergeant was responsible for the safe keeping of the club's arms at all times. He should have realised, in any case, that he was running the risk of getting Choldcroft into trouble; and that wasn't a gentlemanly thing to do. Choldcroft had countered this by defending his club members: it mightn't be gentlemanly, but it wouldn't be that aspect that would enter the head of a young man who thought he could find a better use for the revolver than to leave it lying idly in the club lock-up when it might be more usefully employed in urging the College boat to a much-longed-for victory. Bramley, in his turn, countered this by reminding the sergeant that Travers had by his action laid himself open to the receipt of a summons for being in possession of a fire-arm without having a licence to carry one. He had enlarged upon this by pointing out that this technical slip would give them the chance, if the youth proved intractable, of threatening him with the majesty of the law.

But far from attempting to obstruct the undergraduate had done everything in his power to supply the information of which Sergeant Choldcroft had come in quest. He took him into his bedroom and opened a drawer at the bottom of his chest of drawers.

"This drawer," he said, as he opened it in Choldcroft's presence, "is empty, except for the revolver. I'm not very dressy, and my wardrobe fits quite well into the other three drawers and the hanging cupboard."

But when the drawer was opened, the sergeant, looking expectantly over his young friend's shoulder, saw that not only was the drawer empty of clothes, but that there was not a trace of the expected revolver.

Choldcroft did all he could to convince Bramley that the youth was as surprised as he had been himself. But the London man was sceptical.

"What sort of cock-and-bull explanation did he try to give you?"

"It wasn't a cock-and-bull explanation," said Choldcroft heatedly. "It was the truth—just as much as what I'm telling you now is the truth." He implied that not even by a C.I.D. man from Scotland Yard was he going to be branded as a liar. "He just couldn't explain it—and that's all there is to it. And I believe him."

Travers had explained that he never locked the doors of his rooms: no one in any College ever did. Peterhouse wasn't a den of thieves, any more than any other College, and he trusted his friends. He had willingly given the sergeant a list of the men who were in the habit of visiting him in his rooms. There was Pat

Frimley, of Trinity. He was a third-year man, but he came from Charterhouse, his own school, and he, too, was going, eventually, to West Africa. There were half a dozen men of his own year from Peterhouse—one of whom, Jenkins, also belonged to the revolver club. Lancewood, of Jesus, Perkins, of Clare, and a whole string of other names of men from other Colleges. And Frimley had sometimes brought some other friends of his who were going to start the West African course. They were all interested in the country and liked to talk about it. Ogu Kalawa had been brought along one day: he was dead now, so he didn't really count in the present case. Frimley, too, had once or twice brought along another third-year man from Corpus, Roberts by name, who was trying to make up his mind whether to come or not. Geoffrey Cranston, too, he knew, of Sidney, and another man from Sidney, in his second year, Martlesham from St. Paul's. He presented the full list to Bramley, so that he could make what use he liked of it. All the men had been interviewed at the police station, but none of them could give any explanation of how the revolver came to be missing. They all stoutly denied that they had had anything whatever to do with its disappearance, and Bramley and the Acting Chief Constable had no reason to doubt their denials. They all seemed perfectly normal young men, and there seemed no possible way of connecting them with the crime.

"Things may seem all right on the surface," said Bramley, who didn't like to be baffled. "But as and when we have time we shall have to go into the movements of these young men—all of them," he emphasised, as he turned a suspicious glance on Choldcroft, "and find out just what they were doing and where they were shortly before and after the murder of the Chief Constable."

Both Worplesdon and Sergeant Choldcroft thought that this was carrying unnecessary thoroughness to extravagant lengths. But in the face of Bramley's determination neither of them cared to voice his opinion.

Enquiries at the railway station proved no more fruitful. The early workmen's trains had carried their usual complement of passengers, most of whom were quite well known to the station staff, and no particular traveller by the ordinary morning trains had excited any especial suspicion or notice. The revolver might easily have been concealed in a suitcase. Even had the enquiries been instituted on the day following the murder, Worplesdon had grave doubts as to whether the result of the search would have been any more hopeful. He pointed out that the booking-office window was small. The booking clerk on the other side of it had not much chance of seeing much more than the head and shoulders of the passenger, and he was more concerned in ascertaining that the correct fare had been paid than in making a close scrutiny of members of the public as they appeared at the opening to buy their tickets.

Neither the porters nor the ticket collector who had been on duty that day could give any help, and enquiries at Liverpool Street and King's Cross at the other end of the journey were equally vain. Bramley, though to Worplesdon's way of thinking with no particular justification, began to veer towards a motor-car as the probable means of transport of the criminal to London. For nothing that would assist had been elicited as the result of questions put to the staff of the various coaching concerns whose vehicles plied between Cambridge and London. It was not unnatural to expect such an issue. For the police were unable to give any sort of indication to the men they questioned as to the probable appearance of the man they were searching for.

"If," said the Chief Constable, "we're reduced to supposing that our man made the journey by car, I don't see how much nearer we're likely to get unless something happens to turn up by accident to help us."

But Bramley, with years' experience of cases every bit as puzzling as the one which he was at present engaged in following up, refused to be deterred.

"Don't garages here have to have a licence from the University before they can hire out cars?"

"Only to undergraduates," replied Worplesdon, hoping to persuade his friend from town that it was useless to start such a goose-chase as was in his mind. "And we've got nothing to go on that specially justifies us in believing that it's an undergraduate any more than someone from the town that's responsible for Deepcut's murder."

Nevertheless the indefatigable Chief Inspector cajoled his host into detailing several men to cover as many of the garages in the town as possible in search of the smallest scintilla of the evidence which he so badly needed. Worplesdon, anxious as Bramley to clear up the matter, could not help being secretly rather pleased when the voluminous schedules prepared by his staff began to come in in ever-increasing numbers. A lot of car-hire seemed to be done, and in every case it was possible to get some sort of name and address of the hirers. But that again, as the Chief Constable pointed out, didn't really help very much, as the guilty man, if he had gone to town in a hired car, would scarcely have given his real name to the proprietor. And in scarcely any of the cases which were thus brought to the notice of the Chief Inspector were the car-owners able to give the destination of the vehicles they had let out. They were not bound to ask hirers where they were going. If they had sufficient confidence in them to entrust them with their machines—which were insured—they did not need to be supplied with this additional information.

Whilst all this activity was being displayed by the outside staff, there were frequent conferences at the police station between Bramley and the Chief Constable.

"The thing is complicated by this damned Cambridge custom of not locking your doors in College. As far as I can see, if I were a professional thief, I'd spend an occasional week here with very profitable results for myself. Unless anyone has occasion to ask the porter at the lodge for the rooms of some particular fellow he wants to see, I can't see what check there is on anyone from outside getting into any room in the whole of a College. Of course, he'd have to take the risk of finding the owner in. But it would be quite easy for such a chap to say he'd made a mistake, apologise, and go off to play the trick on another staircase, and so on till he *did* have a bit of luck. And during one or two trips I've made round the Colleges, it seems to be the custom not only to leave the doors of sets of rooms unlocked, but even open—so that an intruder would not even have any trouble in selecting an empty room. Whilst you were busy with other things, I don't mind telling you that I've visited *all* the fellows that young Travers told us had the run of his rooms. Of course even he can't say that he's accounted for *everybody.* He told me himself that he might just as well give me the whole College list—anyway of the freshmen—and that runs into over a hundred."

"And haven't you visited all them?" queried Worplesdon, a certain amount of friendly malice in his tone.

"No," said Bramley emphatically, "I haven't. I just concentrated on the short list. Frimley and Cranston gave me all the help they could. They're older than the rest—at the end of their third year, and as they're going to West Africa themselves when they've finished their course here, they're especially interested to clear the name of the University before they go. They seem to think, too, that as they'll have police duties mixed up with the hundred and one other things they'll have to do when they get out to the Coast, a little preliminary detective work at home, even if it's only amateur, won't do them any harm. But they're not so interested in the murder of the Chief Constable as in those of the two nigger fellows. They seem to be a little sore about the failure of the police to trace them. I told them that when they've had as much experience of C.I.D. work as I have they'll learn to be a bit more lenient with us."

Neither Bramley nor his provincial colleague were able to make anything of the advertisement intended for the local paper, which the editor had put into their hands. And there constantly ran through the mind of the London man the idea that the thing might be a hoax. Hoaxes occurred, of course, all over the country. But Oxford and Cambridge were just the sort of places where such things throve and flourished. They might, as in this case, spring from a perverted sense of what was humorous. But they had to be reckoned with.

For some days there seemed to be a complete deadlock. Try what avenue he might, Bramley met with no sort of success, and he suggested to the Chief Constable that all he could do for the time being was to lend him a man to keep things warm—he hoped in more senses than one—until they happened, by luck or hard work—to light upon some sort of a clue which they could follow up with greater certainty. But there seemed little prospect that his hopes would soon or ever be realised. He was thoroughly sick of the whole business.

When at last he left Cambridge, he pondered over the whole matter as he went home to London in the train. There must, he thought, though the connection was obscure, be some sort of link between the outrages on the unoffending negroes in Cambridge and the attempt on the life of Professor Camberley in Africa. There seemed to be a racial feud at the bottom of both. And the known antipathy of Sir Wedgwood to the coloured man as a student in an English University seemed to provide a link if only, by thought or discovery, someone could manage to light upon it. But even assuming that this hypothesis were correct, there was still the murder of the Chief Constable on Parker's Piece to be fitted into its right place in the fantastic jigsaw criminal puzzle. Or had it any place in that at all? Was it a purely isolated event? A mere coincidence. How could the motives of his murderer be even guessed at? He was inclined, often, to dismiss this case from his mind when he was considering the others. Assuming that the two murders and the attempt and threats against Sir Wedgwood were rooted in some inter-racial vendetta? Then on which side of the picture was the tragedy of Deepcut's death to be placed? The Chief Constable was impartial. It was his business to find out the murderer of those who met their deaths by violence within his jurisdiction, whatever might be the colour of their skins. None but a lunatic could pretend to hold him responsible for the death of Ogu Kalawa and Pompoli merely because he had so far been unsuccessful in tracing their assailant. But, assuming that there were reasons of this sort behind the tragedy, the person to be found was someone demented; and, in addition to that, he must be assumed to be a negro. No other person would fit such facts as were known. But he had received no news, during his visit to Cambridge, of the existence of any such person within the limits of the University town.

King's Cross at last—and very glad he was to see it. He jumped into a taxi and within twenty minutes was back at his desk at Scotland yard. He had scarcely seated himself when an orderly entered with a familiar cablegram envelope.

"This has just come in, sir."

Bramley hastily tore it open. He saw that it was from the African Cable Company. The place of origin was Edwardsville, the capital of Old Guinea.

It was from the Commissioner of Police, and ran:

"URGENT STOP NATIVE ABU BOKARI ALIAS ABSALOM PERKINS DETAINED HERE FOR INFRACTION ALIENS ACT STOP REASON BELIEVE WAS IN CAMBRIDGE OCTOBER STOP POSSIBLE MORE SERIOUS CHARGE TO BE PREFERRED STOP CAN YOU GIVE ANY INFORMATION."

Bramley gasped. Was this, in more senses than one, the missing link?

CHAPTER XXII

THE "C.A.D.S." AGAIN

THE Summer term was over—the last summer term which Pat Frimley and Geoffrey Cranston would see as undergraduates. They had duly scrambled through their respective Triposes, and contemplated taking their degrees before much more water had flowed past the Backs, now looking their loveliest on the hot July afternoon, as they lay with Dorothy Camberley on a cool spot of the velvety green lawn of King's, in the shade of the massive Chapel. Next term they would return again, but it would be as graduates, taking the Colonial Office course before they went out to take up such posts as the authorities chose to allot them in one or other of the West Africa Colonies. They had both stayed up during the Vacation term which had just begun, pretending to do a little preliminary work before the official studies began in real earnest. But Frimley's real reason was rather more personal. The Professor's daughter had lost none of the attraction which she had for him, and in the subject of the Cambridge murders and the vicissitudes of Sir Wedgwood Camberley they had always a subject to which they could revert should the conversation chance to take a more dangerous and sentimental turn.

Cranston professed to be anxious to do all that he could to help the police in their job of getting to the bottom of the mysterious series of tragedies, which had interfered with the usual tranquil academic calm of the old University town. But his companions twitted him, and discovered the real reason for his sudden and unusual predilection for extra study in a desire to taste the delights of Cambridge, at the height of the summer, without any pricks of conscience at the number of weekly lectures he was missing, and neglect of his tutor's reiterated instructions to put on a little extra steam as his ordeal in the Tripos had approached.

"It's a good thing, anyway, that things in Africa seem to have settled down as far as your father is concerned."

As he spoke, Geoffrey Cranston scraped off with his cardboard spoon the remainder of a large-size ice-cream brick.

"Ever since they arrested this man Abu Bokari, or whatever he calls himself, the alarms and excursions seem to have stopped. But Dad seems to be getting pretty weary of the country all the same."

Dolly Camberley, for the past week or so, had had some relief from the constant strain which had obsessed her during the greater part of the past Summer term. There had been a welcome respite from the cables which had had a habit of coming in at all sorts of hours, over the telephone, night and morning, after the attack on Sir Wedgwood which had so nearly proved fatal.

"In his last letter, which came this morning, he really seems to have made up his mind to come home at last. I don't think there was any need for him to stay as long as he has. But you know how obstinate Dad always is."

Both her companions nodded feelingly: they did!

"But the fact that he had been attacked—that he knew that somebody wanted him out of the country, or out of the world—badly enough to shoot at him, made him more so than ever. Now that there's been a certain interval without anything sensational happening, he thinks he can beat a retreat without anyone wagging their fingers at him in contempt. Though why he should bother I don't know. But—seriously—it doesn't seem to me that the 'Cads' have done very much to justify the purpose for which they were formed."

"I believe," said Pat Frimley, with mock scorn, "that Geoffrey has forgotten even why they were ever formed."

Cranston was vehement in his denials.

"I like that. I seem to have done a damned sight more than you. I've had heaps of interviews with the Acting Chief Constable—had one with the Chief Constable himself only the morning before the night he was murdered. And then, over this gun business—haven't I done as much as anybody?"

"I know—I know. Dolly's only pulling your leg. There's no need to get all hot and bothered. It's hot enough without that. But—seriously—we don't seem to have made much headway."

"Who has?" exclaimed Cranston. "It doesn't seem to me that the police have got any farther than us. What's happened, when all's said and done? Two African undergraduates have been murdered—one in the street—the other in his rooms in College. The Professor of Experimental Anthropology has been potted at and very nearly done in in West Africa—in the very Colony from which the two fellows came. The Professor has spotted a man in a crowd in court as looking something like the fellow he says he saw in Brookside on the night of the murders. We've got the evidence of the two fellows who found the man dead in the stream at Brookside—and the constable who came to take particulars—that there *was* another nigger on the scene that night—a nigger whom nobody seems to have remembered until it was too late and he'd got away—back to Africa, as it appears from what has happened since. This chap appears to have been traced at last, and to have been detained out there until the police here can find something against him which would justify his being extradited, or whatever it is you call it when a chap is wanted by the police at home when he's actually in one of the Colonies. An anonymous letter received by your father seems to show that there's an anti-white gang at work in Africa. An advertisement which the editor of the *Cambridge Daily Echo* gets shows equally that there is an anti-black gang at work here in England."

He paused in his narration to see whether his hearers were taking in the summary which he was making. They made no sign that they wished to interrupt or correct him, and he continued:

"Does it strike either of you, my comrades and confederates of the C.A.D.S., that there is a significance which no one seems to have pointed out so far in the Chief Constable being what the Yanks would call 'bumped off' so very soon after he had, partly at my instigation, been going through the lists of niggers in Liverpool which he had received, but of which, up to that morning, he didn't appear to have made any use? It seems to me that there *is* some sort of a link there if we only knew how to lay our fingers on it. Then this revolver business. Of course, it's heresy to say so—but I can't help thinking that the fact that the revolver was pinched out of the rooms of a fellow in College points to the fact that we can't entirely rule out the possibility that it's someone in this ancient University, who ought to know better, who's taking a hand in this—I use the word in its literal sense—bloody game."

"Don't mind me," said Dolly demurely, "if it's for my benefit that you're being so polite."

She had been listening intently to the précis which Geoffrey Cranston had been compiling, as if she wished to be able to point out any weak spots in the narrative which she might chance to notice.

"I should hate to believe that it's someone we might all of us know who's had a hand in wiping out the Chief Constable of the town, and with so little reason, so far as we are able to see. But the fact that the Downing porter isn't able to help points to the fact that it *was* an undergraduate—a graduate even, perhaps—who sneaked that gun. These porters are usually pretty cute at noticing any strangers—except members of their own Colleges and members of other Colleges that they know—who come wandering into their domains and poking about on the staircases."

Pat Frimley nodded his agreement on this point.

"Which all goes to make one think that it *was* a member of the University that boned the blunderbuss. How they'll ever trace who it was, or how he got to London and posted the pistol back here, and the letter to the *Daily Echo,* I can't quite see—except by such a stroke of luck as doesn't very often happen."

"And what are they going to do about the black man who was arrested—detained—in Edwardsville?" put in Dolly. "Isn't there something about 'habeas corpus' or something. Won't they have to let him go again and begin all over again if someone doesn't do something pretty snappily?"

"I imagine they will," said Pat, "especially if the African lawyers are as officious as they make out. But if they really do think the fellow has something to do with what happened here, I don't suppose they'll be too anxious to let him go again—anyway until they've had a reasonable time to make enquiries."

"Have you seen Mr. Worplesdon again lately?" asked Dolly.

"I've seen him—but haven't been able to get very much out of him. He used to be so friendly and all that—let me have a few tips as to what was going on. I don't suppose he's really supposed to do that, and they may have spoken to him about it. Of course, he isn't really cut out for a Chief Constable, and I don't think he draws a very hard and fast line between what he lets out and what he doesn't. Of course, we were bound to be let into things a bit when he was making all those enquiries about the revolver. But I've certainly noticed lately—haven't you, Geoffrey?—that he's much more inclined to keep his mouth shut than he used to be."

"I have—very much so," said Geoffrey Cranston emphatically. "Perhaps the police really have got on to something really tangible at last. They've been long enough doing it."

"And I'm not surprised," said Dolly warmly. "For a more mixed-up affair I've never read about—even in a novel."

And Geoffrey Cranston's guess, though he could not have known it when he hazarded it, was not so very much off the mark. During the next few days Chief Inspector Bramley was seen about Cambridge again—often in consultation with the Acting Chief Constable. He was far less inclined to talk than he had been before. He thought that he had hit upon a clue at last, and he told Worplesdon, in confidence, that an arrest might be made at any time during the next few days.

CHAPTER XXIII

THE PROFESSOR'S RETURN

"YOU'RE right, my dear, quite right. It's not by any means the first time I've been out of my own country. I've always been glad to get back. But never—never before have I felt so thankful to set foot on English soil. We, as a people, are very fond of running down our own country—and our own countrymen, for that matter—amongst friends. But now that I've been to West Africa and—thank God—have managed to return safe and sound—I'm more than ever convinced that if I had to be born again, and were to be given the choice, I'd choose to be born an Englishman. That may sound like jingoism, or whatever you like to call it; but it's nothing more than the truth—as it appears to me."

Dolly was more than thankful to see her father back again, after all the anxious times she had had during the past month or two when he was away on his new duties. There was nothing much wrong with him, from his looks. Indeed, the tropical sun had given his usually pallid face a very healthy tan. His feelings on the subject must have been pretty strong for him to have expressed them as he did that summer afternoon in the familiar drawing-room in Park Terrace as he consumed with avidity and relish the very same sort of tea about which he had frequently, in the past, made such biting and unappreciative comments. His daughter had the courage to draw attention to his change of heart, and he received her banter with a smile. He wouldn't give in at once. It did *seem* nice—and he stressed the verb he chose—

but so would anything after what he had had to put up with on the Coast. Strong tea, badly made by a native cook in a cheap teapot—the good one which he had been foolish enough to take out with him had been carelessly smashed during his first week in Old Guinea—and, worse than anything, odious tinned milk to mix with it. He had even grown not to mind the stuff; but he could realise the difference now that he was home again and able to drink the real thing.

"So one good thing will have come out of this trip of yours."

There was a twinkle in Dolly Camberley's eyes, and the Professor thought that he might be going to be trapped into some damaging admission which might in future be used against him.

"Oh, and what's that?"

"You may find out that your daughter isn't quite such a bad housekeeper as you've always imagined her to be."

Sir Wedgwood grunted, but it was a good-humoured grunt. He was so pleased to be in his home again, to have the company of his pretty daughter, that he had not had time to resume all his old brusquerie of manner.

"And I have—so far as I could with all the trouble that my visit seems to have created—managed to get done a fair amount of the work I went out to do, though unfortunately not so much as I had hoped. I don't, however, propose to go back there again and finish it. I've come to the conclusion that, even in anthropology, it's the onlooker—in the laboratory and the museum—that sees most of the game. I may be a little more anxious, in the future, when I am studying native trends of mind and thought, to find some excuse for what seems to us to be their aberrations, now that I know what a foul country they live in, and how unspeakably uncomfortable are their huts and houses."

There was real disgust and loathing in the Professor's voice. He did not seem to have cured himself of his aversion to the black races.

"But who wants to know what progress I have made or haven't made in the scientific line? I was met at Plymouth by a whole horde of these damned reporter fellows. Do you think that they were bursting to hear the results of my researches? Not a bit of it. All they wanted to do was to be ahead of the other competitive rags in getting more sensational stuff out of me about these Cambridge murders."

"And, of course—being in that frame of mind—you obligingly told them!"

Sir Wedgwood nearly choked. Parts of the piece of buttered toast he had been eating went down the wrong way, and it was some time before he had recovered sufficiently to let his daughter know, coherently, his feelings on the subject of the sensational Press of his country. Dolly took advantage of the remission to go out and fill up the teapot with hot water: she was glad it was the servant's day out. There were many more things which she wished to hear from her father than his well-known and now intensified views on the subject of daily journalism. The interval would give him time to switch his mind off the unfortunate subject.

"Of course," said Dolly, on her return from the kitchen, and before he could resume his wrathful tirade, "there *are* lots of things that I want you to tell me about—besides the results of your work. I can read about those afterwards, when you've had time to sort them all out—in a book."

Sir Wedgwood made a deprecatory gesture.

"There you are, Dolly, just as bad as the rest of them. All you seem to be able to raise any interest in is the subject of these murders. They're long enough off now, and the police don't seem to be any further, from what I saw in the evening paper that I got on the way up, than they were when I left."

"I don't think," said Dolly, "that it's quite as bad as you make out. But I *did* want to hear what they had been doing out in Africa—about this man Abu Bokari, or Absalom Perkins, or whatever he calls himself. From the little that I've been able to find out—and it *is* so very little—people seem to think that may be as important as anything else in clearing the matter up here."

The Professor sighed. He saw that there was no hope for it. His daughter would not be satisfied until she had heard the whole story as far as he was able to tell it to her.

He was able to surprise her by telling her that the man had actually come home on the same boat on which he himself had travelled. Whether he was brought as a prisoner or in the capacity of a witness he was unable to say. The man had travelled third class, and when he had reached Plymouth he had been escorted off the ship by two men in plain clothes who seemed to everyone who saw them suspiciously like policemen in mufti. He had himself, before he left Edwardsville, been asked to confront the man and tell the local police whether he could say that he had ever seen him before. Sir Wedgwood had told the authorities that the man was certainly the same man that he had seen at the "barri" at Mandu when he sat in court with the District Commissioner, and he was inclined to think, from his gait and from his back view when he walked, that he was the same person he had seen in Cambridge, near Brookside, on the night on which Kalawa and Pompoli were murdered. As for his features—that was a different matter. At Cambridge, as he was walking along behind the man, he had naturally had no chance of seeing his face. In any case, as the old song went, "All coons looked alike to him," until he learned better in Africa. Even in Cambridge, from his scientific training, he could say that the man's skull was definitely of the dolichocephalic type. And it was his gait, as he left the African court, which had definitely brought the scene in Brookside back to his mind. The police, for their part, appeared to have had cables from the English force which helped to confirm their suspicions that this particular man might have been in Cambridge, and certainly in this country, at the time of the tragic occurrences of the October term. Of what value this information was to the police he did not know. They had not told him, and he had not asked them. He was not interested. He was, in fact, sick to death of the whole matter. He was not inclined to revise his views on the subject of the undesirability of admitting coloured students to the University. Indeed, he had stronger grounds than ever, and his daughter guessed that his views were not modified by the attack to which he had been subjected.

On that count he was still mystified. He knew that it was a commonplace that the European never knew what was going on at the back of the black man's mind, and any books that he had ever read on the subject only convinced him the more of the futility of such speculations. His consolation lay in the fact that it was equally impossible for a black man to fathom the innermost thoughts of the white man. But why this man, Abu Bokari—if indeed he were responsible, a fact which remained to be proved—had shot at him in the dark as he lay in bed and very nearly killed him—he was absolutely unable to understand. He appeared, indeed, to be some sort of connection of the Chief who was the father of one of the murdered men: though very little could be definitely ascertained even on this point. The Professor could understand that. It would not be in the interests of the Chief to try to discover the identity and motives of a man who might be his relative in such a case. If, as people said, rumours had been flying about which associated his own name with the murders, on the flimsy evidence of his own known prejudices, there was the chance that the natives had got hold of the story in a garbled form and actually attributed the crimes to his own agency. As he reiterated, no one really knew what went on in the black man's mind. But if the thoughts were anything like what his conjecture presupposed them to be, he could only say that the black man's mentality, never very high in his own opinion, lived up to the criticism which he had passed upon it, and justified him more than ever in his own policy of the segregation of white and coloured students.

Glad as she was to see her father again, Dolly began to be a little bored at the long recital which was really more or less of a repetition of the views which she had heard so many times before—long before Sir Wedgwood had ever formed any intention of visiting Africa.

There came a ring at the bell.

"Lord—there's the bell." Secretly she was glad of the interruption which might again put her father's thoughts off the train which they were at present pursuing. She got up and went to the front door and opened it. To her surprise two visitors awaited her: Chief Inspector Bramley and the Acting Chief Constable of Cambridge—both in plain clothes.

"Sorry to trouble you, Miss Camberley. But might we have a few words with you?" It was Bramley who took the lead.

"Why—yes—of course." For some reason or other she felt nervous: she felt that her excitement had caused a flush to appear on her face, and she felt awkward as she answered the request. She must, at all events, disguise the identity of her visitors from her father.

"Come inside. Do you mind waiting for a minute—in here?"

She threw open a door which led into a small room off the hall, next to her father's study—a room which she used herself when she was doing some of the intermittent secretarial work which Sir Wedgwood condescended to give her. The two officers being ushered safely in, she closed the door and returned to the drawing-room.

"Who is it now—interrupting like this at tea time?"

Sir Wedgwood, having started on his favourite topic, did not wish to be cut off in full spate.

"Nothing. I shan't be long. Have you got all you want? It's only two men—about the electric light: we've been having a little trouble with it."

At first the girl thought that her father was inclined to disbelieve her. But he was sleepy and tired after his long journey, and she knew, of old, that when he felt like this, he would soon stretch himself out on the sofa and be thankful enough not to be interrupted for half an hour or more. He grunted, and was swallowing his third and last cup of tea as she went out and closed the door behind her.

"It isn't much we want to bother you with," said Bramley cheerfully but, so the girl thought, a little embarrassed, "But did you ever, to your knowledge, speak to Pompoli or Kalawa?"

"Why, yes," cried Dolly, mystified. "To both of them—once or twice. Once, at the Regal Cinema—you know it?—I was there with a friend—Mr. Frimley or Mr. Cranston, or both—I can't quite remember—and Pompoli was sitting in the row behind. I think one of them knew him and introduced me, and we spoke a few words. Mr. Frimley introduced me to Kalawa. A whole lot of people were there."

"Thank you. Only just one more question at present. We do want, some time, to see your father. But another day will do. I hear he's only just got back."

Dolly was thankful. There would certainly have been a scene of no ordinary magnitude had she been compelled to introduce the police officers to Sir Wedgwood at the present juncture.

"I also wanted to ask you if you knew a Mr. Simpson—Henry Simpson? He's got a place in Petty Cury."

"Do you mean Simpson the hairdresser? Well—I just know him. I used to go to him. But I haven't seen him for ever so long—not since that new shop—Kerrison's—opened a couple of years ago—in Market Hill."

Chief Inspector Bramley turned to his companion.

"I think that's all, Worplesdon, that we want to ask Miss Camberley at present, isn't it?"

Worplesdon, all confusion and shyness, agreed; he wasn't used to calling upon University Professors' daughters, and he was astonished at the way in which his colleague could carry matters off.

"I'm so sorry to have troubled you—but that's all I want at present. I might want, perhaps, in a day or two, to come round again."

Dolly Camberley escorted her two visitors to the door. As soon as she had closed it behind them she began to wonder what line the investigations were taking. For there was no doubt—could be no doubt—that the Chief Inspector's strange query, in a way as yet inexplicable to herself, had some bearing on the matter of the Cambridge murders.

CHAPTER XXIV

BRAMLEY PROGRESSES

"I DON'T think I'd better tell you what's in my mind at the moment. You'd probably think that I'd gone stark staring mad, that this thing had been getting on my nerves!"

Chief Inspector Bramley's appearance belied his words. It would have been difficult, thought the Acting Chief Constable, to find a saner or a more cheerful-looking man in the whole of the British Empire than the London detective on the morning after their joint interview with the Professor's daughter.

"You were certainly right when you told me before we went that you were going to surprise me. I give it up. I just can't guess what you're after or how your mind is working. What on earth can Miss Camberley's hairdresser have to do with the case?" Worplesdon was genuinely puzzled.

"Did I ever say that I thought he had? I merely asked her if she went to Simpson, in Petty Cury. She answered that she used to, but that recently she had been going to Kerrison in Market Hill, There's nothing very mysterious in that!"

"Well, I give it up," said Worplesdon. "I haven't the ghost of a notion what it's all about."

"And I won't worry you with it—till I've got a bit further. Though I may want your help a little later this morning."

"I'm glad it won't be till later on," cried Worplesdon, relieved. "I've got a heavy morning in court. I'm prosecuting and I've got to have a talk to my witnesses before I go in."

"All right," said Bramley. "I'll get along now. I'll come on later on and tell you what I want you to do—if I want you after all."

So saying the Chief Inspector took himself off and it was not till well after midday that he reappeared at the police station. The court cases had taken less time than the Chief Constable had anticipated, and he was sitting in his office relaxing over the morning paper.

"Well—what sort of a time have you had?" He looked up from his paper and anticipated from the other's beaming face that the morning's work had, for him, not been unsatisfactory.

"Fine—thanks. I only hope you've had as easy a time as I. But I doubt it. Dealing with fifteen J.P.s—none of whom is a great expert in the law of evidence—is a bit more of a trial than having a friendly chat with one hairdresser."

"Then Mr. Kerrison was helpful?"

Bramley nodded.

"Most helpful: a very intelligent man, that. He's a regular mine of information about the town. Of course he's a ladies' hairdresser. He seems to be popular with the fair sex, and they seem to gossip as much here as they do anywhere else in this country—or any other that I've ever heard of for the matter of that. But before we go any further, you remember that I told you I might ask you to do something for me?"

Worplesdon groaned inwardly. He hadn't forgotten all the extra work he had had over the interviewing of the members of the Revolver Club only a few days since, and the even more strenuous time he had had in the October term when, on the instructions of his chief since dead, acting in concert with the Scotland Yard man, he and his Force had made enquiries at all the College lodges in Cambridge in connection with the murder of Pompoli.

"Sure," said he as cordially as he could. "Court's over to-day and there's only routine work to be done, unless anything special turns up."

"I shouldn't like to say that it mightn't," said Bramley in warning tones; "that is to say," he added cautiously, "if I'm as successful as I have reason to think I'm going to be."

"And if I might ask—what is it exactly you're after now—the murders of the two blacks or the case of the Chief Constable?"

Bramley did not answer at once. He seemed to be pondering deeply and his brow was puckered. And when he did reply it was in slow and measured tones.

"It's not so easy to answer that," he said. "I've been doing some very hard thinking the last day or two. Actually I've been concerned more with the case of Pompoli and Kalawa. But of course I've always had to bear in mind the other as well. It may sound odd to you—but I've an idea that it doesn't really matter which end we begin; but it's best to start at the one where the clues seem most plentiful."

"Meaning, that you think that the three murders are all mixed up together?" Worplesdon was surprised to realise that his colleague seemed to have made up his mind already on this point. He hadn't, himself, been able to see the slightest trace of any connection.

"If my own theory's right—mind you, it's only recently occurred to me and I've had no real opportunity of testing it—but if I'm right—once we get at some idea of the circumstances which led to one murder, we shall not be so very far from solving the whole puzzle. I think, for many reasons—that for the time being, I had better keep it to myself. It might be rather awkward for you if I told you everything."

Worplesdon was a nervous man, despite his many years in the Force. He felt quite a shock at the other's words and Bramley noticed a tremor in his voice as he spoke.

"For me? Why—you surely don't mean to tell me that you suspect that *I* have had anything to do with any of this?"

Bramley laughed. He reassured his companion.

"My dear fellow, *if* I had any suspicions about you, do you think that I should speak like this to you? Wouldn't you be the last person in the town that I'd think of telling such a thing to?" He laughed heartily and tried to put the Acting Chief Constable at his ease. "No—no—it's not that at all. But there's no harm in my telling you that it was something that you told me that someone had said to you that first started me on the train I'm following up."

Despite the other's entreaties, Bramley was adamant. He would tell the Chief Constable no more than this. He repeated that if he told him the words of the remark, and by whom it was alleged to have been spoken, it might, at that juncture, place Worplesdon in a rather awkward situation. And Bramley felt that he would be more at his ease if he did not know yet exactly what was going on in his mind.

"After all—what I've got in my head at present isn't any more than just a theory. If I were to tell you what it was, you would be bound, whether you liked it or not, to keep on turning the thing over and you might begin to imagine as true things that had merely been suggested to you by somebody else. If I can satisfy myself, as I hope I shall—though one can never be too sure in our sort of work—that I am on the right track and can back up my ideas with some real evidence, *then* you will be able to come in and help me follow them up. Till then I'm afraid I must go to work more or less on my own. There is something you can do for me. I told you this morning, before you went into court, that I might come back later and ask you for some assistance. It's very simple, what I have to ask. I want you to let me see the exhibits that you collected in these October cases."

"Exhibits?" cried Worplesdon in surprise. "I didn't remember that we had any."

"There weren't very many, worse luck, or we might have made a little more progress. But you'll remember that you found, in the open drawer in the desk in Pompoli's room in Corpus, an envelope with a mauve paper lining?"

"Oh, that," said Worplesdon, relieved. He feared that there might have been some other objects which, in the welter of enquiries and searches which had followed the crimes, he might have overlooked. "Yes—I've got that all right. It's in the safe in the C.I.D. office."

"You'll remember that there was something in it?"

"As far as I can remember, it was empty," said the Acting Chief Constable, more surprised than ever.

"It was—practically empty. But it's just the 'practically' part of it that matters now. There was a hair in it—a single hair."

Worplesdon remembered. His conscience was clear. The envelope had been placed in another and sealed before the thing was locked away in the police safe, There had been no occasion to refer to it since. He felt certain that it was in exactly the same condition now as it had been when it had been stored away nine months before.

"Ah, yes—I remember now. There *was* a hair. But what has this got to do with the cases of Pompoli, Kalawa and Deepcut?"

Bramley was mysterious. For one thing, he did not want to give away his theory for the present; for another, he was amused to see the reactions of his country colleague to his mood. He didn't often get the chance of playing Sherlock Holmes: police work, nowadays, didn't often yield such opportunities.

"I'm not ready to tell you—*yet*," he said, slowly shaking his head. "But you might like to help me do a little comparison."

Slowly he drew from his pocket a white trade envelope with a printed inscription on the front. Worplesdon recognised it as coming from Kerrison, the ladies' hairdresser. He opened the paper carefully and drew out a short tress of golden hair, not more than three inches long at most, bound in the centre by a piece of black silk thread, and consisting of not more than a couple of dozen strands.

"Would you mind getting that other envelope—the one that was found in Pompoli's room?"

Feeling decidedly excited, but still quite in the dark as to what the detective intended, Worplesdon went out quickly and was back again with an official police sealed foolscap envelope. He broke the seal carefully and, using a piece of his newspaper as a covering for his fingers, drew out its contents. It was the faintly perfumed mauve-lined envelope from the room of the undergraduate who had met his death in Corpus.

Bramley leaned over the table and examined the envelope carefully without touching it. The grimy finger-prints which had been noted at the time of its discovery were plainly apparent and clearly interested the detective. But it was not with the exterior only of the envelope that he was concerned. Using the same means that the Chief Constable had employed for preventing further marks on the paper, he handled the envelope and shook out the golden hair which it still contained.

"Have you got a lens here?"he enquired.

Worplesdon was obliged to make another journey to the C.I.D. room: his own office was not equipped as a detective bureau and he sincerely hoped that the need for such a transformation would never arise. He wasn't cut out for criminal investigation, and knew it. He was quite ready to leave that sort of job to his subordinates. At length he came back with the article for which Bramley had asked. The London man took it from him and, moving from the window so that the sunlight streamed in directly upon the table, made a careful comparison with the glass between the tress of hair from Kerrison's and the single strand which had been left in the envelope. After a short time he sat up again.

"Have a look yourself," he said.

Having made a careful examination, Worplesdon put down the lens.

"I'm no expert. But it does look to me as if these hairs came from the same person."

"The hair from Kerrison," said Bramley quietly, "comes from the head of Miss Dolly Camberley."

CHAPTER XXV

ABU BOKARI SPEAKS

Bramley refused to tell Worplesdon what he deduced from the comparison of the hair found in Pompoli's envelope and that which he had secured from the hairdresser.

"All the facts which I have myself been working on have been under your nose, too, all the time. I dare say I'm quite wrong: there's many a slip 'tween the cup and the lip in this sort of affair. It would be much better if you, remembering for yourself all you can about these cases, were to think things out and see what conclusion you came to yourself. There's plenty of time: I can tell you that. I *do* definitely suspect a definite person, but at present I haven't got enough evidence to let me jump with any prospect of success. There's a lot to be done before I can do that. But if you just, when you've got the time, think the whole thing out again, on your own lines, and at the end of it come to the same conclusion that I have come to myself, it will be a very great help. I shall know then that I'm not just dreaming—making up a story in my own head that seems to fit the facts as we know them. There's another thing that makes me say there's plenty of time. I don't think the fellow I suspect has any idea whatever that he's in any sort of danger. And he's got a certain amount of support for that theory. He has, again supposing that I'm right, successfully managed to murder three people in the same town—two black and one white—without anyone having the least suspicion of who's at the bottom of things, and I'm pretty certain, from what I've seen of him, that he thinks he's as safe as houses."

Worplesdon was completely mystified. He could not, for the life of him, think how the comparison of Dolly's hair—if the hair in Pompoli's envelope was hers at all—could possibly be of any help to the police in tracing the murderer of the three men. He remembered that Bramley, when they had visited Park Terrace the day before, had asked the girl whether she had ever met Pompoli. He remembered her answer: she had spoken to him once, when in company with two white undergraduates, at a casual meeting when he chanced to be sitting behind her and her friends at a cinema. If it were a clue at all, it seemed a very slender one, and the Acting Chief Constable was absolutely at a loss to see in which way it pointed. And yet Bramley had told him—and he had no reason to suppose that his friend was pulling his leg—that he was just as well acquainted with the facts which had led him to his conclusion as the detective was himself.

He puzzled and turned over the problem in his mind all night, but was no nearer seeing light than he had been the day before, when he had agreed with Bramley that the hair in the undergraduate's envelope and that which the detective had obtained at the barber's came probably from the same woman's head.

"It's often the little things that count in chasing criminals, as they do in all kinds of other matters," went on Bramley. "If we are able to lay our hands on Pompoli's murderer—on the man who did in Kalawa and the Chief Constable—it will be mainly owing to the fact that the careful Mr. Kerrison has acquired the habit of collecting samples of his clients hair, with a view, so he told me, to being able later on, if asked, to get the right tint of dye or whatever they call it, in case some day the ladies might happen to need it. It's also a strange fact that in the case of women as young as Miss Camberley he should adopt this practice. It's in the cases of the older ones that it's more important and likely to be of use. But fortunately for me Mr. Kerrison is methodical. He treats them all alike and keeps complete files of all his customers."

Try as he might, Worplesdon was unable to get any further information from Bramley.

"But for the time being we can forget all this," said the detective. "After all, it may be just moon-shine. This thing's like a jigsaw puzzle. There's all sorts of ends and corners to it and until we've combed every side-alley—I'm mixing my metaphors a bit, aren't I?—we can't hope to have a chance of putting them all together properly. So I'm going to drop this one for the moment."

He delved in his pocket and produced a buff telegraph envelope.

"Here's another end of the stick, and you may be able to help me here, too."

Worplesdon groaned inwardly. He was heartily sick of the whole business and didn't know what it all meant. He could not see what help he had given the big man up to now. After all, even without his assistance and corroboration in the matter of the hair, he could just as easily have satisfied himself by his own inspection that both samples came from the same person and that that person was Dorothy Camberley, the Professor's daughter. Listlessly he took the wire from his companion.

It was from Scotland Yard, and addressed to Chief Inspector Bramley at his hotel in Cambridge.

"ABU BOKARI CONSENTS TO INTERVIEW WITH YOU STOP ARRIVES CAMBRIDGE TO-DAY 2.30 ACCOMPANIED BY CONSTABLE. INFORM WORPLESDON."

Things were moving rather more rapidly than the Chief Constable had anticipated. It was a far cry from Dolly Camberley's hair to the elusive native from West Africa who had at times, for reasons best known to himself, concealed his identity under the name of Absalom Perkins.

"It's one o'clock now. Come round to my pub for a spot of lunch and we'll be back here in good time to meet our mysterious young friend from Old Guinea."

* * *

Lunch in company with Bramley had been a refreshing interlude.

The big man, satisfied that there was something in his own theories and hoping that he might manage, with the help of headquarters, to put together a few more pieces of the jigsaw puzzle, forgot all about business for the nonce. He ordered an excellent meal to which his companion, used to a frugal lunch but feeling the need of something more substantial to sustain himself during the coming interrogation, did full justice, even to the brimming pewter pint tankards of Cambridge ale. Bramley was the best of hosts, and his high good humour and rare fund of good stories soon restored Worplesdon to a more cheerful and sanguine frame of mind.

But as the repast came to an end, and Bramley looked at his watch, he realised that zero hour was approaching and that he would soon be plunged again into further investigations of what seemed to him the insoluble problem with which he and the rest of the Force were faced. But there could be no turning back now: he must go through with it.

"We'll soon be over the top again," said Bramley cheerfully. He did not realise what an uncomfortable effect his words had on his companion. He had served in the war: he knew quite well all that the significant phrase implied. But its import, in connection with the matters with which he was now again compelled to deal, was no less sinister.

The way back to the police station seemed all too short, and Worplesdon immediately noticed an unfamiliar pair of men waiting at the top of the steps. One was obviously a constable in plain clothes: that much was evident from his bearing. But he was not one of the Chief Constable's own force. His companion was a short, thin-faced negro, looking as smart as the efforts of the Two Guinea Tailors could make him, and Worplesdon realised that this was the long expected Abu Bokari. Worplesdon himself was sceptical. The whole thing was, to his own way of thinking, in such a muddle and confusion that he seriously doubted whether the evidence of one man would ever enable them to clear it up. But the issue did not lie in his own hands, and he was grateful for small mercies. "Good afternoon, Palmer. So you've come along with Mr. Bokari—to show him the way?"

The negro's features expanded into a broad grin. He was thankful to the big man for making it plain from the start that he was not under arrest. He was a voluntary witness and as such entitled to respect and courtesy.

"Good afternoon, Mr. Bokari. It's very good of you to come all the way from Africa—and London—to help us. Until I heard that you would be able to tell us something I was beginning to give up hope."

Bramley shook hands with the African, who clearly appreciated the friendly way in which he was being received by the Chief Inspector.

"We may use your office, Worplesdon? No doubt you would like to be with us. You may have something to ask Mr. Bokari yourself?"

The Acting Chief Constable gladly accorded the necessary permission. He agreed, too, to be present when the interview with Abu Bokari took place. After all, Bramley seemed very confident, and though he had himself very small hopes of anything of any importance materialising, he clung to straws now and would be very thankful for some sort of indication that the air of mystery which had hung for so long over the University town was likely to be dispelled.

Bramley, Worplesdon and Abu Bokari proceeded at once to the Chief Constable's office. The plain-clothes man from London was excused further attendance till five o'clock. If everything went well, he might be able to return to London by a train which left Cambridge somewhere around a quarter past five.

Abu Bokari, alias Absalom Perkins, was decidedly nervous. His skinny hands, of a pale brown and finer than those of the majority of his race, seemed to tremble slightly as, at the invitation of Worplesdon, he pulled up a chair to the table and placed them upon it interlaced before him.

His face, too, was paler than Worplesdon would have expected to see in a man born in West Africa. There was no trace of grossness or criminality about his features, and the Chief Constable imagined that, in a more comfortable situation, a gleam of humour would have enlivened his dark-brown eyes. He had an incipient moustache, and his thick woolly hair was divided by an artificially cut parting and flattened down as far as its intractable nature would permit. His clothes were new, and he looked smart and up to date in his neat blue serge suit, the passion of his race for vivid colours being betrayed only by the brilliant pink shirt and collar which he wore, still further embellished by a purple silk tie set with an imitation diamond pin of overpowering dimensions. His fingers were ringed with roughly cut African jewellery, and a silk handkerchief rather floridly embellished with designs in all the colours of the rainbow hung elegantly from the left-hand sleeve of his coat.

"I'm very sorry we've had to trouble you, Mr. Bokari."

The negro smiled. The flattery clearly pleased him. Bramley was inwardly amused at the situation, for he had reason to know that it was only veiled threats of a possible charge being made that had induced him, even at the expense of the Government, to make his way back once more to the country which he had left some months before in a suspiciously clandestine fashion.

"I'm only too pleased to be able to help you, if I can."

"You've been in Cambridge before?"

Bramley shot out the question suddenly. It was best to get this point established at once. He realised, if what he suspected was correct, that if he gave the man time to temporise on this subject, a lot of valuable time might be wasted.

"Yes." The negro answered promptly enough. But the way in which he twined and twiddled his fingers for the next few seconds showed that he feared that unpleasant consequences might follow upon his confession.

"We know, of course, Mr. Bokari, that you were originally in Liverpool. You had a passport in the name of Perkins. You were to be apprenticed by your father—a sub-Chief, I believe, in the Chiefdom of which Mr. Ogu Kalawa's father was Chief—to a Liverpool shipping firm?"

Avoiding the detective's gaze, the young man admitted the facts.

"Why did you—changing your name and not telling your firm that you were going—come to Cambridge last October?"

Bramley was hazarding a chance shot. It was only a police theory up to the present that Bokari actually had acted as he now suggested.

"You see—I know. Perhaps you'd like to tell us your story in your own way. We can't force you, of course. There's no charge against you—except something about an infringement of the Aliens' Act. But even that need not be pressed—in certain circumstances."

The negro clearly understood the purport of his questioner's remarks.

He spoke English intelligibly, though here and there he interspersed his speech with phrases of "pidgin" which his hearers found a little difficult to follow. But the tale which he told sounded plausible enough.

Abu Bokari said that he was twenty years of age. Till he reached eighteen he had been a pupil, sent at the expense of his father, the sub-Chief, to the Government school for the sons of Chiefs in the Colony of Old Guinea. It had been his father's intention, ever since he was a child, to have him brought up to take his part in commerce. The old man had formed the opinion that the best way for an educated man to make money was to go into trade. He knew, from the experience of others around him, that the first essential towards success in such a sphere was a thorough grounding in commercial principles in a reputable European house. When Abu Bokari was old enough to leave the Government school, he was to be apprenticed to a Liverpool shipping firm with which the father had become acquainted, to learn the elements of business on the white man's lines.

To Abu Bokari, though he had never dared to question his father's authority, the idea had never appealed. Other pupils of the school, including Ogu Kalawa and Pompoli, were destined for other and, as Bokari saw them, higher things. They were to go to an English University—Cambridge—and learn to be what their fathers called "gentlemen." The negro idea of a gentleman coincided pretty well with the idea which was held in England before the war—and in certain quarters even after that catastrophe which had done so much to upset the ideas of the older generation. A gentleman, in this view, was a man who did no work with his hands and knew nothing of the baser occupations in life which were founded on book-keeping and trading practice.

He wanted to be a scholar, like Ogu Kalawa and Pompoli. They had gone to Cambridge not long after he had reached Liverpool himself, and if he could get in touch with them, they would be able to help him to realise his dreams. A few weeks of the drudgery of the shipping office confirmed his belief that he was not intended for commerce. Conversely they proved to him that he was meant to be a scholar and a "gentleman." He decided to make his way to Cambridge. There was the question of money. It would have been difficult for him to continue to draw the allowance which his father sent him monthly from Africa without giving a clue to his whereabouts. He saved as much as he could and then, without warning, quitted his lodgings. He realised that the provisions of the Aliens' Act were not very strictly enforced, and had little difficulty in securing lodgings, in his assumed name, in a quiet part of the University town. He was very vague and hazy as to what his next move should be. He would have, eventually, to get in touch with his African friends in the University town. But even this would have to be done with circumspection. He did not know how they would react to his appearance. It was quite possible that, however strictly he enjoined them to silence, they would write home to their parents giving the clue to his whereabouts. His whole plan would thus be jeopardised. His father would hear of his wanderings and, somehow or other, he would be traced and either shipped off home to Africa or, still worse, sent back to the grinding drudgery of the office and its routine which was so repugnant to his temperament. He had thought over the situation and devised a plan. He had had talks with some American missionaries settled in his father's district. They had told him many tales of their country and how it was possible there for the poorest man, who had ambition and grit, to acquire a University training. Undergraduates in the States, even with no means of their own, were able to keep themselves to the end of their course by doing all kinds of jobs, menial and otherwise, during the vacations: the fees they earned enabled them to pay the expenses of the following term at the University they had joined. He would do the same at Cambridge. There were lots of things he could do—he had often helped his father and his wives with their crops—sowing and planting rice, clearing the land of heavy timber and brushwood for tilling.

A few talks with his sympathetic landlady had blasted his hopes in this direction. He had always been given to understand that as rice was the staple crop of his own land, so was wheat that of the English people. There would not be very much difference in the way of cultivation. But he learned, sadly, that agriculture in England was conducted on lines vastly different from those on which it was run in his own country, and he was driven back on other lines of defence.

After a stay of only a few days, wandering about, mainly at night, to avoid observation which might lead to his detection, he came to the conclusion that his Utopian dreams must come to an end. He was in despair.

And then the thought came to him—and he wondered that it had not occurred to him before—that he might seek out Kalawa or Pompoli and obtain from them money or advice or both. They had not been especial friends of his at the school—their fathers were wealthier and more important than his own. But here, in England, things would not be the same. They were all three aliens in a foreign land. He knew, however, that relations were strained between Pompoli and Kalawa. Their fathers had always been considered rivals, and the African was inclined to keep up a blood feud where it already existed. He must decide which of the men to approach first—and quickly too, as his slender resources were coming to an end and he had been unable to find any kind of employment in Cambridge.

He did not dare to call upon either of his former friends in the Colleges to which they belonged. But he kept observation on their habits, and having decided that of the two Kalawa would be the better to approach in the first instance, he made up his mind that the St. John's undergraduate must be the first to receive his attentions. It did not take him long to ascertain that he was accustomed very often in the evening to visit another African student who "kept" down the Trumpington Road. He would leave College after Hall and go straight there, not usually returning until half an hour or so before the College gates were finally closed at midnight. Abu Bokari decided to hang about in Bateman Street each night for a week from eleven onwards till he saw the well-known form of Ogu Kalawa pass the end of the road towards Brookside on his way back to St. John's.

On the third night of his self-imposed watch he was successful. He looked down towards the junction of Bateman Street and Brookside and saw the figure of Kalawa, in cap and gown, hurrying past on his way towards the centre of the town. The moment had come: he would accost his former friend and declare himself. He was desperate now—he only had a few shillings left—and he could not think that Kalawa would deny him the help and advice of which he was in need. He could hear hurried footsteps of a couple of persons coming down Bateman Street behind him. He must reach Kalawa before they were upon him. He did not wish to be observed. Swiftly and quietly he hurried down the street. Kalawa, he could see by the light of the street lamps, was walking in the road, close to the side of the stream from which this quarter took its name. He decided to turn down the pavement by the houses on the side of the stream opposite to that which his quarry was following. If he went quickly enough, he would be able to intercept him before he came to where the road branched off, going to the left into the town and to the right up past the Roman Catholic Church and into St. Andrew's Street. Just as he turned the corner, walking almost parallel with Kalawa, he was aware of another figure going in the same direction, a tall man—elderly, to judge by his gait—keeping to the pavement on the side of the Leys School. He got the idea that this man too was trailing Kalawa. He slowed down, and Kalawa gained on him, still keeping to the edge of the street which skirted the stream. He decided that it was safer to wait. He could judge when Kalawa had reached the junction of the roads. He would stay till the coast was clear and then run swiftly down Brookside and accost the negro at the corner, near the old town fountain. Kalawa had now passed out of sight behind the trees which lined the brook. The figure of the tall white man was out of sight, too. He could hear the two men who had been behind him down Bateman Street coming out into Trumpington Street. He must run quickly now and meet Kalawa at the place that he had chosen. Running as fast as he could, he came to the end of Brookside and turned to the left by the fountain. There was no one there. The figure of the tall, elderly white man, still on the same side of the road, was disappearing fast down the street into the town, past the Fitzwilliam Museum He turned and looked back. Kalawa had not been going as fast as he. What could have become of him? Neither did the two figures of the men in Bateman Street appear. He paused a little, and then, hearing nothing, decided that he had missed his man and must seek another opportunity of encountering him. He walked slowly back along the Trumpington Street. About half-way back towards Bateman Street he saw a little cluster of men by the side of the Brook.

The rest of Abu Bokari's narrative coincided with what the police knew already. But for the first time the identity of the unknown negro whom the policeman had spotted after the commission of the crime was definitely established.

"I believe now that I am wrong," said Bokari at the conclusion of his story. "But I learned afterwards that the man I saw by the Leys School was Professor Camberley. I had heard much about him and his prejudice against black people as undergraduates at the University. Although I had not actually seen what happened, I was sure that he was the murderer, and I determined to avenge my fellow-countryman."

He admitted that he had been responsible for the attempt on Sir Wedgwood in Old Guinea. But he was convinced, now, that his suspicions had been wrong, and he was genuinely sorry for what he had done.

It was not Bramley's business to go into the matter of the attack on the Professor. That had been, or would be, dealt with by the African authorities. He must see to what use he could put this new evidence in the enquiry which he was conducting into the Cambridge murders. And beyond establishing the identity of the mysterious African who had been noticed at the spot where Kalawa was murdered soon after the tragic occurrence, it did not seem to get him any farther.

"I'm afraid," said Bokari, "that that is all I can tell you."

Bramley sighed. He was inclined to believe that his informant was telling the truth. If that were so, it seemed to have been rather a waste of effort and money to bring him all the way from Africa.

"If that's all, I'm very sorry you've been troubled. You've been very candid, and though I don't recommend the habit of potting at Cambridge Professors, however you may dislike their views, no real harm seems to have been done."

"There *is* just one more thing," said Bokari nervously. "I don't suppose it's of much importance. But I think perhaps I ought to show you."

Fumbling in his pocket, he produced a battered tin cigarette-case, rusted and worn—the sort of thing one can buy for six-pence at Woolworth's or receive as a magnificent "free" gift in return for an astronomical number of cigarette coupons.

"When the policeman had taken the body away—I was sorry for the dead man. I went back to the place, quietly, when no one else was there, to see if I could find anything—any souvenir. I found this envelope. There's nothing much in it—only a photograph. But I think the people in it must be friends of Kalawa."

To the astonishment of Bramley and Worplesdon he laid on the table a faded and curled snapshot, which, when examined, showed two figures well known by now to both of them. The young woman and her companion, laying on cushions in a punt moored somewhere off the Backs, were none other than Dolly Camberley, the Professor's daughter, and Pat Frimley, the undergraduate from Trinity!

CHAPTER XXVI

SOUNDINGS

"JUST had a note from Worplesdon. What a bore. Wants me to go round and see him at once."

Pat Frimley was in flannels and a blazer. He had arranged to take Dolly Camberley out on the river. She was ready at the Professor's house in Park Terrace when he suddenly appeared and made his announcement.

"Can't you go to him some other time?"

Pat produced the police message from his pocket. It was in an official envelope and was marked "Urgent."

"I don't see how I can. Lately old Worplesdon hasn't been too keen on seeing any of us. Thinks we're a lot of meddling amateurs. Now it looks as if they think we aren't so contemptible after all. And it doesn't do to take liberties with the police when they ask one to go and see them. Can't you ring up Geoffrey and ask him to take my place? He was lunching at the Red Lion, I know. He won't have left there yet."

"No, I don't think I'll trouble him." She made a little *moue* of disgust.

Pat Frimley sensed some trouble.

"Why? What's the matter? Had a row with him?"

The girl did not seem anxious to speak. But Pat was not inclined to let the matter drop so easily.

"He's a queer chap, at times—and most infernally rude and offhand. But it doesn't mean anything."

"I know," replied Dolly. "He hasn't been rude. I'd rather he had been."

"Why, whatever do you mean?" cried the young man, mystified.

"He came round yesterday evening, just after dinner, and asked me to go to the pictures with him. Something about West Africa. How I hate the name of the place! I'd been doing typing for Dad all day—mostly notes of his West African work. So I said that, if he didn't mind, I'd rather not. He said we'd go somewhere where there wasn't a West African picture, and I agreed. I felt I needed a bit of a relaxation. But Geoffrey didn't seem a bit like himself. I couldn't make out what was the matter with him. And it wasn't till after the show was over, as he was walking home with me, that I found out." She gave a little shudder of distaste.

"He suddenly—as we were crossing Parker's Piece—got all sentimental. Asked me if I'd marry him. Said he'd felt like that a long time, but didn't like to say so. I can't tell you how upset I was." There were tears in Dolly's eyes as she concluded.

She liked Geoffrey well enough, as a companion. But she had never thought of him in any other way. And he had never shown any sign of his own feelings.

"Poor old Geoff! What a nasty shock for him!"

Pat knew that he was certain of Dolly's affections, and he could afford to be generous. Besides, he really liked the fellow. He was just as surprised as Dolly to hear what had occurred the night before.

"Anyway—don't bother about it. It'll turn out all right. I'm not surprised at Geoffrey's being smitten. Of course, he didn't know that we were practically engaged already, did he? And that was your fault, you know. It was you who did not want people to know yet. So you were really asking for trouble."

But seeing that the girl was really moved, he kissed her, and she did not resist.

"Well—let's try to forget it. I didn't want to make Geoffrey miserable. But really, I hadn't any idea that he felt like that—about me. But oh, Pat—how I wish you'd never thought of going out to that horrible country——"

"It's a long time yet—not for over a year. I've got to do the course up here before I'm finally passed. And lots of things may happen before then. And now I really must be off. Worplesdon wanted to see me at once. Bramley's with him and he may be wanting to get back to town. I'll come in again as soon as it's over. There may be time even then to go out on the river. Even if it can't be done this afternoon, we might go this evening. We might ask Geoffrey to come along, too."

"No—not so soon—after last night—please!"

Pat Frimley agreed to do as Dolly wished, and, after another kiss, rushed off straight to the police station.

Bramley was there, as he had surmised he would be, and he hastily made his apologies to the two men.

"It seems to me," said Bramley cheerfully, "that the apologies ought to come from us. We don't want to spoil your afternoon, and you look as if you'd had something in view. But we simply couldn't dispense with you. It's very important."

Without further explanations he produced a wallet, from which he took the snapshot which Abu Bokari had found at the scene of the murder of Ogu Kalawa.

"Have you ever seen that before?"

Pat Frimley flushed with excitement, and his change of colour did not pass unnoticed by the two policemen.

"Why—yes—of course I have."

"Do you remember where it was taken, and when, and also who took it?"

Bramley's tone was kindly.

"Why, yes! I do. It was taken last year—on the Backs—in the summer term. Cranston and Miss Camberley and I were out together in a punt. Cranston had a camera—a new one—that he wanted to try, and that was the first snap he ever took with it."

"And Kalawa and Pompoli—both Cranston and yourself had a nodding acquaintance with them, I believe? Would Cranston have been likely to give a copy to either of them?"

"I should think," said Frimley, "that that would be most unlikely. Why should Kalawa or Pompoli have wanted it, anyway?"

"Neither of them had expressed any admiration for Miss Camberley?" prompted Bramley.

The young man reddened.

"I introduced Miss Camberley to Kalawa one day—I can't even remember where. He was certainly struck, I should say. But he was a most quiet and unassuming fellow. I don't think he'd have dared to get fresh with a white girl or to want to have her photograph."

"And Pompoli—the other one?" went on Bramley. "From what I remember of the enquiries we made he wasn't quite so unassuming. He wasn't unknown to take girls—of a sort—out to dine in town?"

Pat Frimley agreed. Everybody in Corpus knew that, and both he and Cranston knew a good many fellows in that College. They had heard it, too.

"And I believe I am right in saying—am I not—that Pompoli, too, had been introduced to Miss Camberley?"

He saw that his visitor was nervous: that he could not understand to what end the questions were being directed.

"Look here, Mr. Frimley, I'm not trying to trap you. The matter has not, I assure you, got anything at all to do with you. I have had a certain theory in my mind for the past day or two, and it has now been backed up with some facts. Some of the things that you may be able to tell me will perhaps be very important corroboration. I want you to try, please, to answer my questions as accurately as you can. You will have guessed, of course, that I am still seeking a solution of the Cambridge murders."

There was nothing more that Bramley had to ask, and Frimley departed completely mystified as to the course that things were taking. He had the satisfaction of noticing that the Acting Chief Constable of Cambridge was no less puzzled at his colleague's line of action.

"Can you spare me one of your men—for an hour? I don't think it will take any longer."

Worplesdon indicated his assent.

"And would you get your man to put me through to the lodge of Trinity College?"

The call was put through and Bramley took up the receiver. He got in touch with the porter, and asked him whether it would be possible for him to supply a full list of the men who had attended Professor Camberley's lectures during the October term and any time before. There seemed to be some difficulty about this. A roster of names was kept at the door of the hall which students attending were expected to sign. But the porter had no faith, so far as Worplesdon was able to gather, in the accuracy of the document, even if it had not, as most likely would be the case, been destroyed. Bramley hung up the receiver, but he did not seem unduly disappointed.

"If you'll excuse me a minute," said Worplesdon, "I'll just go and have a word with the sergeant and see how we are off for spare men this afternoon."

He went out, and when he returned some minutes later Bramley was again at the telephone.

"You're certain," he was asking of the voice at the other end of the line, "that those are all the Sidney men who went to these lectures?"

He appeared to be reassured as he again hung up the receiver.

"Well now," said he, "I'll leave you to yourself for a time. I'm sorry to have been such a nuisance. But I think I can assure you that before very long you'll be left in peace again, so far as I am concerned, and as far as the matter concerns the Cambridge murders."

Before the other had had time to recover from his astonishment the Chief Inspector was out of the room, requesting Worplesdon, as he closed the door, to send the constable he had asked for to follow him to Sidney.

* * *

It was five o'clock in the evening before Bramley returned. He seemed tired but jubilant, and he took his time about filling and lighting his pipe and settling down to make himself as comfortable as possible in Worplesdon's official visitors' chair.

"I take off my hat," said he at last, "to the College porters of Cambridge."

It was a remark which the Acting Chief Constable was ready to endorse; but he failed to see its exact relevancy in the present circumstances.

"I mean," went on his companion, "the way they keep their records of the comings and goings of the young gentlemen in their charge. Even if they haven't got the actual lists any more, their memories are so good that they are able to give a policeman a wonderful lot of useful information."

He was interrupted by a knock on the door. A constable entered with a telegram.

"For me?" queried the Chief Inspector. "I was expecting a reply from London."

The orderly handed him the message. He opened the envelope, read the contents of the wire, folded up the paper with a sigh which sounded like one of relief, and put it into his pocket. Worplesdon wondered at his reticence.

"I'll explain this later," said Bramley, tapping the pocket into which he had put the paper. "It will come in better when I have finished what I was going to tell you."

"You'll remember, I dare say, telling me that you were in the room one day—this room—when your predecessor was trying to trace the identity and whereabouts of the young man whom we now know as Abu Bokari—and that young Cranston came in to find out how things were progressing?"

Worplesdon nodded.

"You'll remember your surprise when Deepcut, who didn't seem to have made much progress up to then with these crimes, said that he had a new theory—a theory that the murderer of the two black men was not a black himself, but a white man?"

Again Worplesdon nodded.

"Of course, I don't know what Deepcut was thinking—he may just have been covering his own ignorance in the presence of an undergraduate amateur detective who was showing more keenness on the job than by then he had begun to feel himself.

Anyway—in my opinion—*it was those words that sealed his own doom.*"

Worplesdon gasped.

"But how?"

"Who was in the room when he said that?" asked Bramley.

"Why," said Worplesdon, more mystified than ever, "only Cranston, Frimley and myself."

"And I don't suspect you or Frimley," retorted the other.

"Then you mean to say that——"

"Geoffrey Cranston is the man who was responsible for the deaths of Kalawa, Pompoli and the Chief Constable, and, indirectly, for the attack on the Professor."

He broke the news to the astonished Acting Chief Constable. Before, he had been working in the dark. When he knew the consequence which had followed the remark which Deepcut had made, he was able, for trial purposes, to single out a particular person whose actions could be traced and reactions noted. That person was Geoffrey Cranston. Once he had got a starting-point he was able to follow up his enquiries with a definite end. He had not expected such luck as had fallen to his lot. That very afternoon he had had an interview with the porter at Sidney Sussex College, who was able to say that Geoffrey Cranston, on that memorable November night, had been out of College from soon after Hall until a few minutes before midnight. He had come in breathless and panting, and the porter recollected that he had smelt of spirits and had been drinking quite as much as was good for him. Enquiries as to the night on which the Chief Constable had been murdered were still more enlightening. Cranston, leaving the College again soon after Hall, had told the porter that he had an exeat to London on urgent business and would not be back till some time the following day. To prove his story he had shown him the exeat signed by his tutor. The porter was able to tell Bramley that Cranston kept a small two-seater car at a garage in St. Andrew's Street. Enquiries that afternoon at the garage had proved to Bramley that on the night of Deepcut's murder the young man had told the keeper that he would be going to London very early the following morning, soon after dawn, and asked him to be ready to let him have it out. Scenting an extra fee, the proprietor had agreed to his request, and it was he who, early next morning, had delivered the machine to its owner. Cranston carried a small brown-paper parcel. He did not return till late the following night, and the porter at the College was again able to corroborate that the undergraduate had not returned to Sidney Sussex till shortly before midnight.

But the question of motive was still missing. He must have some almost insane complex about the black races. Further enquiries showed that he was one of the men who attended Professor Camberley's lectures. He was also a candidate himself for service in West Africa. Bramley knew, from what Worplesdon and Deepcut had told him, that the young man was frequently seen about in company with Dolly Camberley and young Frimley. It was not impossible that he had been smitten with that very presentable young woman's charms. Bramley had noted the colour of Dolly's hair, and he remembered having seen a strand of similar hair in Pompoli's room when the examination was made after his murder. Had the negro student, whose amorous tendencies had been revealed, been making advances in Dolly's direction? The comparison of the barber's tress with the hair in the envelope lent some colour to the suggestion. They now knew that Dolly had been introduced to Pompoli at a cinema and that he had been sitting directly behind her. Had he, in a sentimental mood, possessed himself of some hair from the young lady's head, and did Cranston, full of jealousy and racial animosity, come to suspect this? It certainly seemed, from the state in which the negro's desk was found after the murder, that the murderer, before committing the crime, had made his victim search for something in the drawers. And it looked as if he had himself taken something away. What he had abstracted might be the rest of the hairs which the amorous negro had surreptitiously removed.

They knew that Dolly had met Kalawa, and that she had not been unfavourably impressed. Did Cranston see in the other African a possible rival? Not, of course, in the serious sense of the word. But, combined with the postulated racial complex, here might be sufficient cause of offence to the jealous swain.

It all seemed insane, as Bramley admitted, but many murderers *were* insane in one way or another, or they would not become homicidal. Bramley was merely stating what he had discovered. There was ample opportunity for Cranston, on that dark November night, to ambush himself in deserted Brookside, and, unseen, to make use of the small automatic pistol of which he had got possession somehow, to make away with Kalawa. There was no one very near at the time; Professor Camberley was on the other side of the road: the two undergraduates coming from the station had not yet, as they knew, by then turned the corner of Bateman Street, and Abu Bokari had admitted that his own view of the scene of the attack was obscured by the trees. There was ample opportunity for Cranston—if it were he—to make his get-away. He had already, according to Bramley's theory, disposed of Pompoli. Enquiries at the College at the time of the murder had shown how easy it would be for anyone to come in as a visitor, climb the deserted stair, obtain admittance to Pompoli's room, murder him, and get away as quietly as he had come, without attracting the notice of the porter or anyone else.

"I don't suppose," said Bramley, "that if Deepcut hadn't made that remark in his presence, and put him, without any real reason, in fear of discovery, we should ever have solved, as I believe we have, the mystery of the Cambridge murders. Once I had got so far I didn't find any difficulty in seeing who it was who had abstracted the revolver from the room of the fellow in Peterhouse. The bullet which was found in the punt was a spare one dropped by Cranston. He had been careless, as so many murderers often are—especially mad ones—about the little things that eventually matter. You will remember that it was known that Cranston was one of the fellows who were in the habit of visiting the owner. Abu Bokari, of course, was barking up the wrong tree. His strange notion that it was the Professor who had bumped off his compatriots was shared, I'm sorry to say, by a few short-sighted people over here who were foolish enough to suppose that because the old boy had strong views about black men in white universities he'd be such a fool as to put them into practice by weeding out a few in Cambridge on his own account!"

"There are a few things to be filled in yet," said Worplesdon, staggered at the recital to which he had listened, and loth, even yet, to believe it. "I suppose your next step will be to apply for a warrant of arrest for Cranston?"

Bramley drew the telegram from his pocket.

"I don't think," said he quietly, "that that will be necessary. The reason I wanted to borrow one of your men was in case I had trouble. I wanted to be sure of my man. At the College I found out where Cranston might usually be found in London. The porter said he looked rather queer. He seemed to have had a shock or a disappointment or something last night. He went to London this morning. Read that."

Worplesdon took the paper from Bramley's hand and read:

"BRAMLEY, POLICE STATION, CAMBRIDGE. WATSON JUST RETURNED BAYNES' CLUB SOHO REPORTS CRANSTON FOUND SHOT IN ROOM BY SMALL AUTOMATIC STOP DETAILS AS SOON AS POSSIBLE BY PHONE."

"It's the best thing that could have happened. I'm sorry myself for the poor blighter. But it's just as well for our West African friends to know that it wasn't a sane man who acted as Cranston did. But I think that our friend the Professor will have to be a little more careful in future about the remarks he makes at his lectures and in the Press."

* * *

It was a strange story which Dolly Camberley read in the paper next morning, and the Professor was strangely silent. She asked to be excused and went to her room, and when she came down at luncheon-time her eyes were wet with recent tears. She said little until Pat Frimley called to see her that afternoon. There was no point in going over the whole sad story. They knew that Cranston, who was usually a cheerful enough companion, had fits of depression and strangeness, and the girl felt partly guilty on account of the incident which had happened two nights before.

"Poor Geoffrey! I'm sorry. When he was himself he couldn't have done anything like that—or spoken to me the way he did. But oh—Pat—don't—don't go to that dreadful country!"

It was a big decision to take in so short a space, affecting as it did the whole of one's future. For the moment he promised to think the matter over, and silenced Dolly Camberley with a kiss—a kiss which the girl felt made up for a lot of the agonies of torment which she had suffered.

Printed in the United Kingdom
by Lightning Source UK Ltd.
135989UK00001BA/124-126/P

9 781906 288075